Of Butterflies & Bullies

Of Butterflies & Bullies

By Jenny Dalton

Of Butterflies & Bullies by Jenny Dalton

Published by Love in Action Press, 780 Vichy Hills Drive, Ukiah, CA 95482

ISBN: 9781798843772

For permissions contact:

Jen@kitchentableconsulting.com

Cover by Colored Horse Studios.

First edition.

This book is dedicated to all the bullied girls out there. You are not alone. You are not broken. You are beautiful, whole and full of possibilities. Hold your head high. Start journaling. Speak only kind works to yourself. You are strong. You are constantly evolving and changing, just like the caterpillar and the butterfly.

With gratitude to the Wiry Goats, Rebecca Brams, Lisa Crovo Dion, Alexandra D'Italia and the women of *Defenestration*, Laura Nilsen, Jody Handley and the late, great Frederick Mead.

"Depicted in symbols and art since the Bronze Age, butterflies are among the most fascinating and beautiful animals. They live nearly everywhere — from gardens and mountains to acid bogs and arctic tundra. About 10,000 to 20,000 species occur worldwide; of these, almost 700, including occasional strays, are found in North America north of Mexico."

– National Audubon Society Field Guide to Butterflies

1

The summer before fifth grade was like every summer before it. I got to swim anytime I wanted at the swim club we'd belonged to since I was a baby, I played softball at the little league and I spent almost every day with my best friend Nicole.

We loved to play school out of any other game we thought of because we had a whole collection of real teacher's materials. My Aunt Sally was a teacher and she let us have all her old attendance books. Sometimes we'd make up names for our pretend students, but usually we just used the ones that were already in there. We especially loved teaching our separate classes but coming together during breaks to gossip like Mrs. Marsh, our fourth-grade teacher did with Mrs. Roach, the second-grade teacher. Almost every day, Mrs. Roach knocked on Mrs. Marsh's door when we were in the middle of a lesson and Mrs. Marsh would say to us "read quietly to yourselves class, I'll be right back." Then she'd take a folder from her desk and hold it up in front of her face and lean out the door to chat. They whispered to each other from behind the folder. Everyone in class tried to hear what they were saying, but we never could.

Chatting behind folders was our favorite part of playing school. We also liked organizing stacks of papers, taking attendance and disciplining the bad kids. Colin, my little brother, wouldn't play school with us anymore because me or Nicole was quick to scold him for any movement that didn't fit in with our plan, "Colin, sit down and put your head on your desk and think about how interrupting the class has disrupted the lesson and your classmates."

Since Colin wouldn't play with us, we taught all two of my Barbies plus a stuffed bear, a stuffed dog and a stuffed parrot in our makeshift classroom in my humid back yard. Sometimes, Nicole brought her six Barbies over so we could have bigger classes. She brought them over in a clear plastic bag decorated with strawberries. I loved that bag of hers.

Aside from a round black grill in our yard, my parents had some old, plastic lawn furniture that we set up to create a walkway and desks for the students. Nicole and I made ourselves comfortable at our mock desks, mine was an overturned cooler and hers the side of my dad's red toolbox and busied ourselves making class lists.

"I've got two Stephanies this year," I said. "They're both blond and I can never tell them apart." I flipped through the attendance roster and wrote down the name Orlando, imagining a kid from my class last year who always got into trouble.

"Shh." Nicole held her finger to her lips and smiled at me. "My class is in session. They are working on the math problem I have on the board."

We didn't have a real chalkboard outside, we just pretended.

"Whoops. I'm sorry," I giggled.

Nicole giggled too and we'd go back to teaching our individual classes. We liked to tease each other.

After those afternoons we played together at my house, I'd ask my mom if Nicole could stay the night if her mom said it was okay. If we were at Nicole's house, or her mom picked us up from the pool, she'd ask her mom. We knew we really didn't have to ever ask anyone's permission. We'd sleepover at each other's house since we were in second grade, but we always asked anyways.

The summer nights were pretty quiet in general. Often a bunch of us kids ranging in age from six to 12 would be out playing tag or hide and seek, even at dark, until one of our parents would start a much-hated chain reaction that would send us all back to our homes for the night. This one night, about a week before we went back to school, was especially quiet since a lot of people were out of town visiting relatives or at someone's lake house up north. My family never went on vacations. Once we went to Tennessee to camp near a lake with some of my parent's friends, but I was too young to remember much besides trying to take a pee behind a tree when no one was looking. No, our summers were spent at home, in the neighborhood. And, especially since my mom was pregnant, she didn't want to go anywhere.

When my Dad got home from work, we all ate grilled hot dogs with watermelon for dessert at the table on the front porch. As it got darker, lightening bugs lit up the lawn and in the neighborhood street. We watched them from the screened-in porch.

"They won't be around much longer," Dad said and sipped on his beer.

Mom rubbed her hand over her belly. "The baby kicked." She said to Dad. He reached over to touch it and us kids let the screen door slam behind us.

Running around the yard capturing lightening bugs was a sport for us. Colin was the most competitive and carried a Bell jar with him so he could count and collect. He'd punch holes in the lid with a screwdriver and Dad's help so they could breathe. I just liked to hold them in my hands and watch them wander around in my palm. I always let them go. And, Nicole did the same. We liked to do the same stuff.

Colin ran up to me, breathless with a trickle of sweat on his forehead. "I've got five," he said, and screwed the top onto the bell jar.

"Way to go," I said like my softball coach always did when we got a hit. "I've got one." I held the lightening bug in my hand and watched it buzz its wings. It flew off and left a yellow powdery residue on my palm. I wiped it on Colin's shirt.

"Mom," Colin yelled, "Molly wiped bug juice on me."

I gave him a pinch on the arm and put on my teacher voice. "Shh. Put on your nighttime voice."

Nicole was over in the next-door neighbor's yard chasing more fireflies and I called to her. She caught up with us in front of the porch. A glow from the driveway light switched on over us.

"I had a few, but I let them go." She wiped her sweaty hands on her shorts then grabbed my hand. "They're just gonna die in that jar," she said to Colin.

"No, they won't. I'll let 'em go before we have to go inside."

I felt the heavy air on my face and sweat on my arms and legs. "I'm ready to go sit in front of the fan. Maybe Mom bought ice cream."

"Let's go check," Nicole swung my hand with hers and we skipped towards the porch as Colin released the bugs into the night sky.

Mom called us inside. She'd anticipated our need of ice cream and had three bowls and spoons out on the counter in the kitchen. Dad sat on the brown couch in the living room watching TV with a bowl in his hands, shoveling it in.

We fixed our bowls in the kitchen and brought them with us to sit around his legs on the floor. Mom joined us a few minutes later with a bowl for herself and we watched Donnie and Marie Osmond sing about being a little bit country and a little bit rock and roll. Nicole and I sang along.

When it was time to go to bed, Nicole borrowed one of my oversized t-shirts. I had a whole bunch of adult-sized shirts that Dad always picked up at construction supply stores. They had prints of backhoes and John Deere tractors on them and since Dad preferred to wear only white t-shirts, I kept them to wear to bed because they were so soft.

Nicole and I slept in my bed together head to toe. This is how we always slept because she rolled around a lot while she slept, and I had a twin bed. When we slept at her house it was better because she had a bed big enough for two people. My window was open to just the screen and I could hear the television over at our other neighbor's house. A younger couple lived there, and we didn't see them much.

When Nicole stayed over, we talked late into the night. We liked to talk about what our lives would be like when we were older. Nicole's big dream was to marry a rich man and have lots of babies. Sometimes she said she wanted to be a cashier at Marsh, the local grocery store. I thought being a cashier would be fun because you got to hold money all the time and press buttons on the register. Plus, you could say hello to people all day and get to know folks in the neighborhood. But I didn't want to wear a green apron all day and, besides, I wasn't so good at math.

"I'm gonna be a teacher," I said, "And, I'll live in the country and teach in a schoolhouse just like on *Little House on the Prairie.*"

Nicole sat up on her elbow and leaned her head into her hands, "Last week you said you were gonna be a photographer in New York City. Which is it?"

"I can have more than one dream." That photographer dream was because Mom took me to the art museum, and I saw a lot of black and white photographs of buildings and people. Mom told me she had a friend who was a photographer in New York City and that gave me the idea. I wanted to make pretty art that hung in museums. But that was last week. This week I was into *Little House on the Prairie* and Laura Ingalls. She was silly and ran through the fields and always did what was right. We got to watch a lot of TV.

"We're best friends, right?" I asked her, just because I thought about it.

"Always,' she said with her wide smile. "And, when we get married, you'll still be my best friend."

"And, when we have babies, they'll be best friends too."

"Even our baby's babies will be best friends. We'll all live across the street from each other and everything."

I gave Nicole a light pinch on the arm that we both knew meant a sisterly version of "I love you."

Yep, the Indianapolis summer was just like any other since Nicole and I became best friends. But, sadly, it was the summer before everything changed and we had to go to a new school because we were special. We were going to a new school because we were smart.

2

One week later we practiced silly putdowns over at Nicole's house. We learned to say put downs from a boy down the street and thought they were just the funniest things we'd ever heard. We sat face-to-face on the black pleather ottoman in her den and shot insults back and forth. The chair was like a black ship in a sea of brown shag carpet. I rocked back and forth clutching my stomach trying to hold in my pee. I always peed when I laughed too hard.

"Okay. I've got another one. Your mom is so small, she plays handball against the curb," Nicole said between laughs. The fan behind her blew her hair into her face and she pushed strands behind her ear, one after another.

"Ooh, burn. You got me." I watched as Nicole's forefinger sizzled against her own backside. We erupted into another round of deep belly laughs.

"Girls, girls. Settle down. Now I see why Mrs. Dean asked you to leave the Brownies troop. You two are wild childs," her mom said as she brought two glasses of ice-cold, fresh-squeezed lemonade for us. It was true. We'd been "asked to leave" our troop last year because we got "lost in their own world." We "giggled too much," Mrs. Dean said. We "didn't pay attention." We "made our own rules." We didn't even like Brownies anyways.

I thought Nicole's mom was so pretty. She looked perfectly tanned in her short white shorts and bright green shirt, like she just got back from playing a game of tennis, but really, she'd just come in from her gardening. Her shoulder-length blond hair had plump heavy curls and she wore her large sunglasses like a headband over her hair. She liked to tease us.

"I hope you learned a lesson and will behave more lady-like at your new school. I don't think your new teachers will appreciate the interruptions. Plus, remember you're being sent there because you're smart, not because you are hooligans."

"No, Mrs. Carr, we'll behave. We promise." I said, speaking for us both and nodding in Nicole's direction. She held in her laugh so that her cheeks grew puffy.

We took our lemonades onto the screened-in back porch and sat down on the lounge chairs that had pretty pink peonies on the white cushions. They were so soft and comfortable; I felt like I could melt into them.

A warm breeze melted the ice in our drinks, and I got the chills when I took a sip. Goosebumps rose up my arm. I watched Nicole sip on her lemonade as we sat in silence and listened to the grasshoppers in her backyard. I heard the sound of a lawn mower in the distance and it made me drowsy.

"What do you think our new school will be like, Molly?"

"I don't know. Different. I guess."

"Yeah, I suppose there will be all kinds of new kids and people we don't know."

I figured Nicole liked meeting new people even though her family didn't go on vacation over the summer either; they did like to take trips to ski in the winter and she said they always met new people when they did that. I never really got to meet too many new people, except in books or on TV, when we got new teachers or at softball. But all of those people lived in the neighborhood and my family liked to hang out in our neighborhood

"Yah." I said. "I know, it's weird. We have to get a ride to school, too. I've been walking to 55 since I can remember."

"Me too."

"Duh. We've been walking together for like forever," I reminded her.

"We'll have to think up new games to play on the way home from school."

Nicole and I liked to make up games as we walked with our moms home from school. One of our moms would meet us at school and let us walk on our own so we could walk in baby steps the whole way, or extra-large steps, or skip over the cracks in the sidewalk. Every day we tried something different.

I felt something funny bubble in my stomach.

"I'm kinda scared," I said to Nicole, my voice almost a whisper.

"Me too." She smiled. We'll be fine."

Barney, the Carr's golden retriever came onto the porch and I let him smell my hand. Then I stroked his head. Nicole grabbed one of her mom's magazines from a rack next to the lounge chair. We looked at the clothes and I tried to imagine myself wearing the same things as the models. I saw a picture of a woman wearing a dress with a big red lobster on it. I showed it to Nicole.

"You should wear a dress like that for the first day of school," I teased her.

"Yeah. And, you can wear a dress with a big red rooster on it."

"We'll be the wacky twins."

"The wacky twins, I like it. That's us."

We sipped our lemonade and I smiled. I was so lucky to have a friend like Nicole.

Later, at home, I sat on the front porch, read and enjoyed the cooler air of the day. I was happy to be alone and *The Secret Behind the Wooden Staircase,* one of the 15 Nancy Drew mysteries I'd inherited from my mom, was really good. Nancy was always a brave detective who wasn't afraid of ghosts or weird noises in the dark. She drove around her town in a blue convertible and encountered mysteries that needed solving. When I read Nancy Drew stories, I liked to daydream that I was Nancy. That it was me that helped my neighbors learn that the problem had an easy solution – that you just had to hunt around for it. In my dreams, the neighbors always told me I'd done a really good job and a few times I imagined I won the key to the city from the Mayor because I solved the toughest mystery in town. But, most times, I imagined that Nicole was with me and we did it together and that we'd both get a key to the city.

When *The Secret Behind the Wooden Staircase* fell and hit the floor, I realized I'd been daydreaming again. I did that a lot. I even got a bad mark on my report card in second grade, when all you get is either a 1, 2, or 3 in every subject, just because I "spent too much time staring out the window." I didn't care though. I liked to daydream because it gave me all kinds of great ideas. And, this daydreaming session gave me a really good one. I'd write a diary and keep it as a secret pal to share my deepest secrets. I would write all my observations and feelings. My secret journal would be my way of recording my new life in fifth grade with my wacky twin and having a secret all my own.

I had the perfect diary in my room. I loved my room because it was all mine and covered in butterfly posters, flowered wallpaper in pinks and greens and matching drapes. I had a pink comforter and pink pillowcases, too. And a stack of my favorite books was on the floor next to my bed and Mom never asked me to pick them up and put them on my bookshelf.

I threw a bunch of old comic books and puzzles from my desk until I found it. The diary was red leather and had a lock. My Grandpa gave it to me for my birthday when I turned nine, but I was too interested in *The Lion, the Witch and the Wardrobe* book he gave me to notice or remember it, until now when I wanted it most. It was right where I'd left it.

I grabbed a pen, opened the diary to the first page and began to write:

Dear Diary,

You are a new friend. I'm almost ready to start my first day of 5th grade at a new school in a different part of town. I guess I should tell you a little bit about myself. My name is Molly Ann Greely and I'm 10 years old. I live in Indianapolis, Indiana with my mom and dad and little brother Colin. My best friend is Nicole Carr. I love to read books and ride my bike. It's almost the end of summer now.

Well, that's it. I'm hungry and want to see if Dad's making hamburgers tonight, I promise to write more soon. Love Molly.

I locked the diary and put the key in the secret compartment in my ballerina jewelry box. I put the diary back into the desk under old issues of Highlights that were way too young for me and promised to write in it every day. It felt good.

The Sunday afternoon before school started, we went to Kmart for supplies. Luckily the station wagon was out of the shop – it was there a lot.

The air conditioning was broken, again, though, and I wondered if my thighs would stick to the plastic seats, permanently.

"I'm so sick of summer, Mom."

"Me too sweetie. Just be glad you're not six months pregnant. I'm hot for two of us."

I laughed, hung my right arm out the window and leaned my chin on my hand. I watched the neighborhood lined with maples, oaks and elm trees pass by us. I closed my eyes and thought that in exactly 17 hours, I'd start school as a fifth grader. I wondered what the new kids would be like. Would I like them? Would they like me? And who was my new teacher?

"Hey dough-dough brain, we're here," yelled Colin from the backseat.

The three of us walked across the hot parking lot into the ice-cold store. It was my favorite time of year – time to buy school supplies. I loved to get organized and choose a different color notebook for each subject. This year I was especially excited because I was finally allowed to bring my own paper to school. No more of that flimsy brown writing paper with the wide lines. I was ready to use the kind of notebooks the high school kids had in their three-ring binders.

The school supply aisle was crowded with moms and kids last-minute school shopping like us. Spiral notebooks and packages of pencils and pens lay in piles on the floor. Chaos and leftovers filled the aisle.

I chose a green notebook for Math, my least favorite color for my most hated subject; red for social studies; blue for science and yellow for language arts. I really wanted the Strawberry Shortcake Trapper Keeper™, with a colorful outdoor scene and butterflies flying around a blue sky; but chose the plain blue one instead. I wasn't sure what the other kids were interested in at my new school. And, since I was going to be in fifth grade, I figured I was getting a bit too old for Strawberry Shortcake anyway. I figured I could always decorate the blue one with stickers. I chose a packet of butterfly stickers from a selection hanging on the wall. This set had a bunch of natural looking butterflies that looked like the monarch butterflies on the posters on my bedroom walls. I loved butterflies and thought they were more beautiful than any other creature on the planet.

Last Spring, I saw a cocoon on the wooden fence that separated our house from our neighbors. For weeks I watched it get bigger and bigger until one day the cocoon was empty. When summer came, what was left of the cocoon eventually fell away from the wood. But I never forgot about the butterfly that was born in my yard and sometimes wondered where it lived.

Back home, I organized my school supplies into piles, so I was ready to bring them to school. Mom made us all a big dinner of roast chicken and carrots, my favorite. Mom and Dad let us watch one hour of TV before we had to go to bed to get a good night sleep for the first day of school.

I couldn't sleep, so I turned on my light in the middle of the night to finish my Nancy Drew book. I think I was nervous to start at my new school. Maybe I knew something big was going to happen in the new school year. But maybe I just couldn't sleep.

3

Mom yelled at me to hurry up the next morning and it sort of upset me. But I couldn't help it; for the first time, my clothes seemed to be the most important thing and I took a lot of time to choose my outfit. Usually, Mom picked my outfit for me, but I was too old for that now. I was an official fifth grader.

"You shoulda picked it out last night," she yelled just as I tied my shoe.

I wore a light cotton sundress with spaghetti straps and my red Keds. I carried a Nancy Drew lunchbox filled with a baloney sandwich on white bread, green grapes and lemonade in a thermos. My mom always packed good lunches.

Usually I just walked the two, short, tree-line blocks to school with Mom and Colin. But School 84 was in Meridian Hills, the rich neighborhood, and my mom and Nicole's mom had to take turns driving us there.

As we traveled to the school, Nicole talked to her mom. I didn't catch any of what they were saying. I was preoccupied with my thoughts and watched the houses grow larger and larger. It's not like I'd never been to Meridian Hills before, our swim club, was there. I'd just never known anyone who lived over there. So, I never really compared the two.

In our neighborhood, all the houses were right next to each other with maybe ten houses on each side of the block. They seemed all neat and tidy like houses on a Monopoly board. But on Central Street, w. school made a huge dent with its largeness, there were only five hous ⌐r block. Most were made of brick, unlike the mostly wooden or plastic siding homes where we lived. These homes had ornate, carved, matching shutters on all the windows – upstairs and down. Each house had a yard that was big enough to play hide and seek and never find the hiders. There were lots of trees, shrubs and flowers and long driveways that went to garages that were all the way back around the houses. In our neighborhood the garages were attached to the house with just the shortest gravel driveways.

School 84 was large, brick and matched many of the houses that surrounded it. It looked old not in a battered way, but in an imposing, I'm an old school way. It was on a corner, across the street from a Catholic church and co-ed school called Immaculate Heart. Students wearing identical green and blue plaid uniforms and white short-sleeved shirts chased each other outside. I was glad I didn't have to go to a Catholic school. Wearing a uniform looked so boring. I loved that I got to pick my own outfit.

A teacher greeted us, looked at a sheet attached to a clipboard and told us to go to the second floor. We climbed a wood and marble staircase and looked down at the students below and I realized I'd never been in a two-story school. It made me feel older.

"Sweet. This is like high school," I said, and Nicole laughed.

I felt good when I walked into the new room and saw neat rows of desks, hardwood floors and books lining the walls. There were so many books I felt like I was in a library – one of my many favorite places in the world. I loved to go to the downtown library and wander through the tall stacks of books in the back rooms of the enormous limestone building.

My excitement grew and I caught myself jumping up and down. A girl with dark brown hair gave me a look, but I didn't stop. I skipped over to a desk that had my name on it – written in red marker on a piece of folded construction paper. I guessed we were sitting in alphabetical order because Nicole was a few rows in front and a boy named Will Halverson sat directly behind me.

Everything was so nice and looked new. The floors were old and creaky, but they were polished. In our old school, some of the window blinds were torn and our pet frog, Rocky, looked tired. Here the sun shined bright through the windows and I watched as all the kids found their way to their seats.

Some of the boys in the class wore white oxford shirts tucked into corduroy pants; others cotton short-sleeved shirts with alligators or horses on them. I had no idea what these symbols meant. The boys at my old school wore tee-shirts with sports team logos on them. A handful of the girls wore skirts with button down blouses and silver barrettes held their hair above their ears. I ran my hand through my short hair and wished I had long enough hair to wear barrettes like that.

"Welcome students. Settle down please."

The room went quiet, the teacher turned to write her name on the board and a kid to the left of me burped. We all laughed.

"Please" said the teacher in a tone that was both pleading and direct. "I'm Ms. Byers. That's Ms. Byers. Not Mrs. or Miss. Please address me accordingly. Let me tell you a bit about myself. Then I'll tell you about my plans for you this year.' She paused to look each of us in the eye.

"I once swam in a lake inside a volcano. My uncle invented the automatic icemaker. I personally met two presidents and I love to camp. Raise your hand if you enjoy falling asleep with the stars over your head and waking up with the dew of the day."

I smiled and raised my hand and remembered peeing by the tree. I counted five boys and one girl raise their hands.

"Very good. Now. This year will be an adventure – a grand voyage of your senses and your mind. I plan to take you on a journey to the pioneer days, to a time when young boys and girls, much your same age, journey across the Western plains to new lands. I'll take you to deserted islands and on voyages with dogs. And, we'll meet some very interesting people along the way. So, who's with me?" She looked at each of us, individually, right in the eye again. Her body bent forward. She beckoned us with her eyes.

"Are you?" she asked stopping at the desk of a girl who wore bright red ribbons in her pigtails. The girl nodded and looked down at her desk.

"And, how about you?" she asked a blond boy who giggled and fidgeted as she walked toward him.

I listened to Ms. Byers and my heart beat fast. It was all I could do not to stand up and wave her over – come talk to me! Ask me if I want to go, I do, I do. But it didn't feel like the right time, so I stayed quiet.

"Are any of you wondering how we're going to get to all these amazing places and meet all these interesting folks?" Ms. Byers walked to her desk and grabbed a very large open book. It was so big she struggled to hold it in her arms. She looked like she might topple over from its weight. She glanced around the classroom. A fly landed on the windowsill.

We looked at her with puzzled faces.

"We're going to read about them! We will read over six novels this year." Ms. Byers clapped the book shut. I heard a couple of groans behind me. "What I have here is a dictionary. And, every day, one of you will choose a word at random and read the definition to the class. This will become our word of the day."

I bounced in my seat at the sound of her voice – reading and new words couldn't thrill me more. I was in heaven. I loved books and discovering new places and learning about all sorts of people. I couldn't believe my luck.

"And, we're not only going to do a lot of reading this year, we'll also make dioramas, keep a reading journal, and at the end of the school year, each of you will present a ten-minute talk on a topic that you choose. We'll spend a good part of the first half of the year on how to become critical thinkers and research information so that just after the winter break, we'll be ready to begin with the final talk. We'll also present one mini talk of three minutes just before the break. How does that sound to all of you?"

I heard a lot of "Ughs. Groans. Sighs." Many of the kids didn't like what they heard. I was elated. This really was going to be so different from fourth grade where all we did was math problems on the chalkboard and memorize spelling words.

At lunch, I sat next to Nicole in a crowded lunchroom. There were long metal tables with metal benches attached with metal hinges. The lunchroom looked like the one at my old school except it was in the basement. When we walked single file down the stairs to give our milk or lunch money to the old woman sitting at a desk collecting it, we had the pleasure of walking past the boiler room and a cave-like room with a door. I don't know where the door went, but I got shivers down my spine and the hair on my arms pricked up as I walked past.

Nicole and I chummed around, shared our sandwiches and giggled about our teacher. "She's so excited," Nicole said. We mixed our chips and grapes into the foil from one of our sandwiches and dug in.

At the table next to us sat a group of girls and boys from our class that we hadn't really met yet. Sure, we'd gone around the room and said our names at roll call, but I thought it was so weird that I didn't' really know their names yet. That they were so new to me was just weird – just like Nicole and I had predicted.

"They're probably all friends from fourth grade, like us," I said to Nicole as I bit into my baloney sandwich.

"Probably," Nicole said with her mouth totally full of grapes. I laughed so hard I almost choked.

There were four girls and three boys at the table. They all had clear plastic baggies for their sandwiches and chips, instead of foil like us. Besides the baggies, they looked different and I couldn't quite put my finger on it. They all seemed older than me. They dressed in pressed cotton collared shirts and jeans – the boys and the girls – and the girls all wore silver barrettes to hold their hair up above their ears. As a group, they had a comfort that I'd lost between the excitement of meeting Ms. Byers and sitting down to lunch.

At our old school, I was the one who knew everything – the best spot for doing tricks on the bars of the jungle gym, the sweetest spot in the shade for Chinese jump rope and I could distinguish between all the mean and nice teachers. I walked to and from school and everyone knew my brother and me. They knew my friends and that I could make it to the second to last round of the spelling bee.

I realized these kids were from this neighborhood. They were the rich kids who lived in the big brick houses set away from the road. Suddenly, I felt more different than I'd ever felt.

Nicole snagged the last of grapes.

"Hey." I said. "You've already had your share."

"So," she tried to pop them in her mouth. When she missed, they flew across the room behind her.

We laughed, deep from our bellies.

The sun shined bright through the basement windows. Nicole wiped her mouth with the corner of a napkin and pretended to be all proper and dainty. She giggled. I smiled and felt happy because I knew everything about her and the same way she knew all about me. I knew she was allergic to chocolate and she knew I told the silliest jokes.

I looked back at the table of rich kids. A few of them watched us. Two boys, Mark and Kevin, gave us the most attention. Mark had sandy brown hair cut really close to his head. I thought he looked like he might be a bully with the boys. But not like the fat kid bully who stole your lunch money – there was a kid like that when I was in third grade and he was weird because he brought a dried-up flattened frog body in for show and tell. He said his brother stepped on it and then they let it dry on the back porch. Nicole and I thought it was so gross.

No, Kevin was different. He had blue eyes and was cute in a mangy puppy dog kind of way. He wore his longer brown hair in a no style, style; mostly it looked like he had run a couple times around a dusty baseball field, did a few hundred sit-ups in the dirt, and wiped himself off too quick before coming to school dressed in pressed pants, sneakers and a red collared shirt. I shot them a take-a-picture-it-will-last-longer-look.

I smiled at Nicole. "Ms. Byers is really different from Mrs. Marsh, huh?"

"Yeah, she reminds me of my grandma. In a good way."

"My grandma never swam in a volcano," I said.

I wanted a different reaction from her when I mentioned the difference between Ms. Byers and Mrs. Marsh. She just seemed better and I wanted her to notice it too. Like she really cared about us learning. I'd never felt that from a teacher. I didn't think Ms. Byers was the type to gossip with a folder over her face or leave us to read to ourselves so she could close the door and go into the hallway. But I didn't say anything to Nicole because I couldn't figure out how to say what I wanted to say. It was something new that I didn't have a word for, so I just finished my baloney sandwich.

The girls at the other table looked at us again. The girl with dark brown hair down to her shoulders who'd looked at me funny when I first walked into our classroom, Melissa, whispered into the ears of the girls on both sides of her and they all laughed.

Nicole looked over at them and looked back to me. I shrugged and kicked her ankle from under the table. She looked up from her egg sandwich, which smelled so strong I thought I might puke, and gave Melissa a really big smile that didn't seem like a real smile at all. I wondered what they were laughing about, but I didn't think it was anything that we did. I wondered if we'd ever be friends with them.

By the end of the day, I was sweaty from the heavy heat that filled the room. My sundress stuck to my thighs and my socks drooped down around my ankles. A fly buzzed by and landed on the desk to my right and the boy next to me shoed it away with a swipe of his hands. He was taller than the other boys, some of whom were shorter than me; and Nicole and I were the shortest girls in our class. He had blond hair, blue eyes and wore a crisp white button-down shirt like the kind my Dad wore to work, but with short sleeves. He wore corduroys, even though it was about 80 degrees and muggy, and he didn't sweat at all. As a matter of fact, he looked perfect. Not a hair out of place, not a bead of water dripping from his forehead. Unlike some of the other boys, Ms. Byers hadn't had to ask him to settle down or be quiet. He kept to himself all day.

When the bell rang at 3:15, school was over for the day. In Mom's car on the way home, I asked Nicole about the tall blond boy in our class.

"Mike Spangler," she said. "He's so cute."

She kissed her hand like she was in love with it, then tried to get me to kiss her hand.

"Ewww," I said. "Stop that."

When we were in fourth grade, a girl from our class named Julie walked home with this boy Andy sometimes, and I heard they kissed in her backyard once. I thought it was pretty gross and guessed that Julie's older sisters taught her how to do it. Even if I had older sisters, I knew I wouldn't want to kiss a boy until at least high school.

In third grade there was this girl named Renee who had a boyfriend in our class. His name was Allen. No one ever talked about them or told other people that they'd seen them kissing or holding hands or anything. I never saw them even talk to each other. It was just known that they were boyfriend girlfriend. I just thought this was so weird. In the movies and on TV, boyfriends and girlfriends kissed and hugged and ate dinner and walked in the park together. Even Mary, Laura Ingall's sister, had a boyfriend and they kissed on the show. And, I guess that's all right. But, having a boyfriend in third grade just seemed silly to me. But, now, thinking about Mike Spangler and his blond hair, I felt differently for the first time. I didn't want to kiss him or anything, but the idea of touching his hand made my stomach feel really funny – like there was a lump of mud in there. I wondered if Nicole wanted to kiss him.

Nicole was staying at my house until her mom got home from work. Mom had a plate of fresh baked lemon cookies and lemonade out on the porch for us. I was so happy that Mom did stuff like that for Colin and me. And, I was so proud to share that kind of stuff with Nicole.

"Well, now that you're done playing kissy face tell me about your first day."

"Good," I said and put a whole cookie into my mouth at once. Mom sat in one of her wicker chairs and rubbed her hands over her belly. Drops of sweat dotted her arms. She took off her shoes and reached for her book that was facedown on the table.

Nicole nibbled on her cookie after she drank half her lemonade in one gulp. "Our teacher wants us to call her Ms. not Miss or Mrs."

"Yeah. Her family invents things and she camps," I said. "She told us we will do lots of talks this year."

"What do you mean, talks," Mom took a cookie too.

"You know," I told her, "like we have to research a topic then make a talk about it."

"We don't know what the talks will be about yet. We're supposed to find out soon after we get into our reading groups." Nicole said.

Mom went into the house to wash the dishes and left Nicole and me on the porch with the plate of cookies. "Save some for Colin," she yelled through the screen door.

I didn't worry about that. I was full from just three cookies and rubbed my belly.

"Look at me. It looks like I have a baby like Mom." I pushed my belly out as far as I could, so I looked pregnant beneath my sundress. Nicole laughed and I let my stomach fall back in to me like a balloon that lost all its air.

"The talks sound scary," Nicole said. She hopped down from her chair onto the green porch carpet and laid down on her back and put her feet up on the chair seat. I joined her.

"Why," I asked. Our heads touched and she sighed.

"I don't know. I don't want to read a report in front of the whole class." I thought about the time we had to sing a few minutes of our own songs in a melody at the school-wide Christmas show last year and how Nicole reacted when the teacher asked for her to sing a few lines from "Frosty the Snowman." Nicole tried to remember the words without looking at the sheet of music, just like Mr. Otto asked, but she couldn't. She kept messing up and stopped a few times because she couldn't remember the words. She told me afterwards that she never wanted to sing in front of the class again. Maybe she thought giving a talk would be like that too. I wanted to make her feel better.

"At least we don't have to memorize it. I heard in high school you have to memorize 15-minute speeches."

"Who told you that?"

"Your mamma."

We giggled.

After Nicole went home, we all sat down as a family for dinner. Mom made chicken potpie, one of my favorites. I loved to watch as she removed the little tin foil bowls from the oven and poured the chicken potpie contents into bowls for us to use. Since it was the first day of school, Mom and Dad wanted to ask me and Colin about our new teachers, so we all sat at the dining room table together, at the same time, instead of eating at different times. Usually, during school time, me, Colin and Mom ate together, and Dad would have his dinner when he got home later.

Mom smiled at me as she flicked out her napkin and laid into her lap. I could see my body in her green eyes. "Well," she asked.

I foosed on my potpie to make it cooler. My grandpa came up with this term "foosing," when Colin and I were little, and he told us we had the power to control the temperature of our own food. Foosing has been a special word in our family ever since.

"What's your new teacher like," he asked again when I didn't answer right away. I indicated that I had hot food in my mouth by huffing and pointing at my tongue.

"You've got seafood," Colin laughed. He picked out the peas in his pie and took a bite. "You know, see, "he stuck out his tongue to show us the crushed-up food in his mouth, "food."

"Don't talk with your mouth full," Dad told Colin.

"Her name is Ms. Byers and I really like her. She's really nice and I think she might be really old. We have to read a lot of books this year, but I think it'll be fun. And, there are all kinds of new kids in my class."

"What schools did they come from," Mom asked. She buttered a slice of Wonder Bread for each of us and passed them out.

"They don't come from other schools. They're from 84, I think. I mean, I didn't ask or anything, but I think they are all friends from forever. You know, like me and Nicole."

"Were they nice to you," Dad asked. His plate was already empty. He always finished first and usually got seconds. But when we had chicken pot pie there weren't seconds because Mom usually only bought enough for us each to have one.

"I guess," I said to Dad. "I didn't really talk to them or anything."

"What does Nicole think," Mom asked.

"I don't know. Why don't you ask Colin about his day?"

"We will," Mom said, "but you're the smarties pants in the new school. This is a big deal."

"I know," I said in a whine. She always told me I was a smarty pants. I hated that.

"I have Mrs. Marsh this year," Colin said. He smiled and I noticed he had a milk mustache and decided not to tell him about it. It was so funny.

"Molly had her last year. She should like you since Molly got good grades in her class," Mom said. I said "Duh" to myself so no one could hear.

I finished my dinner and decided I'd rather find something to wear to school and write in my journal than watch tv with Dad and Colin. I asked to be excused in my best imitation of Laura Ingalls. I wanted to see if I could find an outfit to make me look more like the girls today. For some reason I couldn't identify, I had to look more like them.

Dear Diary,

I love my teacher Ms. Byers because she is very nice and doesn't gossip to other teachers. I'm at a new school and there are kids who I am just getting to know. This is new for me because I'm used to going to school with the same kids since 2ⁿᵈ grade. There are some nice girls in my new class, I don't know them very well yet. And, a tall boy named Mike Spangler I think is cute.

The next day at school, I sat up straight in my chair when Ms. Byers began to tell us about reading the word of the day. I wondered if she'd choose us alphabetically or just close her eyes and put a finger on a name in her grade book. It was neither. She had a big cowboy hat on a table next to her desk and she asked each of us to write our names on a strip of orange construction paper and put it into the hat. After I threw my name into the hat, I pulled my favorite blue Strawberry Shortcake t-shirt to cover my lower back (I didn't have any shirts like the girls yesterday) to hide my underwear.

I watched as Ms. Byers stirred the names with her right hand while everyone put their names in the hat. At one point she looked right at me and

I looked her in the eyes and smiled. There were rays of wrinkles next to her eyes that grew deeper when she smiled. They made her look soft and I wanted her to call on me, to pick my name out of the hat so I could be the first to read in front of the whole class. She smiled back and nodded. I took this to mean she understood where I was coming from – that I wanted to participate.

Once everyone had their names in the hat and Ms. Byers was confident she'd stirred them all up well, she picked one. A shy girl named Jane went to the front of the room, her head down. Jane was different from the girls at the lunch table – the rich girls. Her clothes were too big for her body and she wore big, round tortoise shell glasses. The entire room was silent as she opened the huge dictionary, closed her eyes, and picked a word at random. "Pathetic. Do I have to read all the definitions?"

"Just one is fine dear. Excellent question," Ms. Byers moved her chair closer to her desk.

"Pathetic," Jane continued, her voice shaky, "so inadequate as to be laughable or contemptible (informal)."

"Thank you, Jane, you may sit down now."

Ms. Byers waited for Jane to find her seat before she asked us to use the word in a sentence. Kevin, the one who looked like Pig Pen from the peanuts cartoon strip, raised his hand and yelled out, "My brother is a pathetic UNO player."

"That's quite good Kevin, anyone else?"

"The tennis match was pathetic," said Bret, a blond boy who was bigger than the other boys.

"Another great use of the word pathetic. Anyone else?"

I tried to think of a good sentence. I wanted to show Ms. Byers that I was a good student and I really wanted to say something smart or important, but I was frozen. I couldn't think of anything. What was pathetic, I thought, was my inability to come up with a sentence. But I knew I couldn't say that.

Later at lunch, I sat with Nicole again. The rich girls, Lisa, Melissa, and Kelly sat across the table from us this time. I told Nicole it was pathetic that her Mom didn't pack her crumb cakes. We laughed. The rich girls didn't laugh. They just talked to each other.

Mark and Kevin sat at the table behind us. I heard Mark tell the table that Jane was pathetic. I didn't know if anyone else at my table heard him say it, but I didn't say anything. I thought it was really mean. I thought that Mark was so mean, and I could tell I didn't like him because I got a funny feeling in my stomach and didn't feel like finishing my sandwich.

At recess, Melissa asked us to play Chinese jump rope with her, Lisa and Kelly. I loved Chinese jump rope and knew all the songs and tricks. Nicole and I played it all the time at our old school, sometimes with a girl named Yolanda and sometimes, we'd just put the rope between one of us and a chair so we could practice. I was so glad the rich girls finally asked us to join their group because I thought it was so pathetic for us all to sit at lunch together and never talk. We had to become friends somehow and even though I didn't need any new friends, I thought it was just too weird not to know all the kids in your class. But, since we were new, I didn't know how to ask them to do anything, so I was glad Melissa was the one who asked us first.

Nicole and Melissa held the rope around their ankles, and we all watched and sang along as Kelly did some tricks. I was amazed that we knew all the same songs. I don't remember anyone teaching me to do Chinese jump rope, I think we just taught ourselves. But it was really neat to know we all had it in common.

I leaned back on my palms and let my head fall back between my shoulders as I sat on the grass. I was relaxed and happy and my worrying about not having a sentence was long gone.

"Your turn Molly," Kelly said.

"To jump or to hold?" I asked as I wiped my hands on my skirt.

"Jump," Nicole said and smiled up at me.

I jumped through the rope and twisted as I jumped again. I could do this with my eyes closed, so I did. I was almost done with my third set of tricks when I heard Melissa say, "My turn."

Nicole and Lisa let the rope go slack.

I could've jumped forever, but I figured it was time to give someone else a chance. So, I put the rope around my ankles and held the rope with Lisa while Nicole took a break with Kelly. Before she sat down though, she whispered something in my ear I could barely hear with all the kids screaming and running around the playground, but I thought she said, "That was kinda pushy."

4

Megan's mom invited the entire class over to their house on an October Saturday afternoon for a party. I'd never been to a boy and girl party before, except when it was Colin's birthday and all his friends came over for cake and pin-the-tale-on-the-donkey. But Colin's friends weren't real boys; they were little boys.

Over the first weeks of school, I started to notice the boys in my class like never before. Like, I noticed that Mike Spangler always bit on the end of his pencil when he was thinking really hard during math. When I was bored, I watched him. When it took Ms. Byers forever to explain the parts of a story we read to someone who didn't understand it, I watched him. When Lisa struggled with her answer to a social studies question, I watched him. Sometimes I ignored Ms. Byers' instruction to watch him. And, it wasn't because I was always bored by the subject matter or anything, it was almost like I couldn't help it. Even if I tried not to watch him, I did anyways.

And, then there was Will. He was tall and goofy. He had the same laidback way of dressing nice like Mike Spangler, Mark and the other boys, but he had a loud laugh that just came out of him real natural. Sometimes he laughed out loud when nobody else was laughing. He just laughed to himself, at something he thought was funny. I liked that about him. And, so did most everyone else. He never got teased for it.

Because of my new interest in boys, I had a hard time deciding what to wear to the party at Kelly's. Nicole and I discussed it all morning and went over the possibilities on the phone. Her mom bought her a new dress, so she didn't need help. I hadn't seen it yet, but since my mom didn't offer to buy me a new dress, I didn't ask to see hers or ask Mom to go shopping. Shopping was something Mom did during special occasions like Christmas, birthdays and the beginning of the school year. She wasn't a casual shopper like Nicole's mom who liked to go to the mall almost every weekend just to see what they had. My mom thought shopping was like a chore, not a fun activity to do with her daughter. She preferred to show me her latest crocheted pillowcase or listen to a record or read a book more than she liked trying on pants.

I got one new dress at the beginning of the school year and I'd already worn it a few times. I wanted something that felt special and new, but since I didn't have anything, I had to make something up out of the shirts, skirts and pants I had in my closet. I choose a wrap jean skirt that made me feel country like Laura Ingalls and a white turtleneck with blue whales on it. I wore a pair of lace up brown boots that I loved to complete my look. I felt good.

Mrs. Carr drove us to the party. Nicole wore a red gingham dress with a bow around the waist. I felt a little underdressed, but there was no time to change.

When we got to Kelly's most kids from class were already in her backyard. I figured they had to all live close by and probably walked there. I wondered if we were the only kids who lived in another neighborhood.

Kelly wore jeans and a brown collared shirt decorated with white horses with a white ribbon tied around the collar. Melissa and Lisa looked similar, but their shirts didn't have horses on them, just flowers and patterns. It made me feel not so underdressed and happier to see them.

Nicole and I went to the patio to get cans of Coke from the cooler and I noticed that Kelly, Melissa and Lisa wore the same kind of jeans. Each jean had a loop sewn onto both back pockets. I whispered to Nicole about them.

"They're Calvin Klein." She whispered back.

"Oh," I said, "How do you know that?"

"My mom just bought me some," she answered as she reached into a big red cooler to grab a soda.

I didn't want to think about how I didn't have a new pair of jeans, so I looked around the yard. Melissa and Lisa were sitting at a table by the pool and I watched as they looked out of the corner of their eyes at Kevin and Mike Spangler, who lounged with Dr. Pepper's on deck chairs.

Kelly's house was huge. Probably the biggest house I'd ever been in. They had a back deck with three levels. On the first level were built-in benches along the sides and a patio table with an opened blue and white-striped umbrella in the center of it. The umbrella went all the way through the big table, which could seat eight people, and was the nicest backyard table I'd seen outside of the swim club we went to every summer. The second tier had a built-in barbeque. In the winter, my dad always put his grill in the garage until the snow melted and the weather got warmer. This grill was a permanent fixture on the patio and was closed-in with brick and took up almost an entire side of the patio. On the lower level, was a hot tub connected to the rectangular pool that took up most of the backyard. And, even though it was sunny but not hot anymore, just almost chilly and almost fall, the pool had an empty blown up raft in it.

"I tried to get my Mom to have a pool party so we could all swim, but she didn't want the liability," Kelly said when she came up next to me.

Kelly's mom, like a lot of the moms of the girls in my class, had a real job just like her dad. She was a lawyer, so Kelly always used words like liability and litigate even when we were on the playground – not just in class to impress Ms. Byers.

I heard Nicole's laugh behind me and noticed she'd joined Melissa and Lisa over by Kevin and Mike. I guess she thought I was busy talking to Kelly because I didn't even hear her ask me to join her.

"I love your pool. Do you swim a lot?" I asked, feeling like an idiot because I didn't have anything funny to say. I wanted her to like that I was a funny person, but I also didn't know if she was a funny person, so I didn't feel too bad. We had been going to school together for almost a month, but I only knew the school Kelly. I knew she liked to draw horses on her notebook.

"Duh. Only when I'm not riding, though."

"Wow. Do you have a horse?"

"Yeah, but he lives in the country with my Grandma. His name is Sweetness. I visit him in the summer and sometimes on weekends."

"Neat." I felt like a dork. I didn't know what to say to her. How can I compete with a horse? I didn't even have good Barbies.

"Let's go over there," I said and pointed to Nicole and the rest of the group.

I didn't know what else to say and I realized it had been a long time since I had to make new friends and, sadly, my diary didn't count. All my friends at my old school were people I'd known all my life and kids from my own neighborhood. It wasn't like I had to try to be their friends or anything.

"I think she wears a bra," Melissa said as we approached.

"That's why her clothes are so baggy," Lisa said.

"Who are you talking about," Kelly asked.

"Jane," all of them said at once.

I looked behind me. Jane sat by herself with a paper plate of macaroni salad on her lap.

"I saw her at the mall with my mom. She was in the bra department," Melissa said. She put her right hand in the back pocket of her dark blue Calvin Klein jeans.

"What were you doing in the bra department?" I asked. I looked Melissa in the eyes and waited for an answer. She giggled and Nicole shot me a look.

"Bra," Melissa said and snapped the strap now visible under her own shirt. I thought it was funny how you notice things more after you know about them. They take shape and meaning when they are known. The bra straps were unmistakable.

Lisa, who was clearly flat, looked away. Kelly smiled.

"Me too," Kelly said.

"Wow" Nicole said. "Since when?" She moved closer to Mark and Mike Spangler, even though they were now talking really loud with Bret, Kevin and Will.

"Since the beginning of the summer," Kelly said as she pushed her breasts up toward her collar.

"Let's see," I said.

Kelly didn't look like she had boobs from the outside of her clothes. She unbuttoned the front of her shirt a few buttons so we could see her white bra straps. I felt funny inside. She and Melissa were the first girls I knew to wear a bra. I thought it would be awhile until I could wear one because I didn't even have bumps yet. Nicole did. We saw each other naked all the time when she stayed the night. And, I was never jealous when I noticed her bumps got a little bigger. I didn't want boobs. I didn't want to wear a bra. I liked my chest the way it was. But Kelly and Melissa were showing me whole new side of it. They were proud.

During the rest of the party I was very aware of my chest. I wondered if everyone could tell there was nothing between my nakedness and my whale turtleneck. I felt like I was missing out on something.

Kelly's light brown pigtail braids flopped behind her as she led us girls up the stairs to her bedroom, like a tour guide, to show us her collection of ceramic and wooden horses. She displayed the horses in a line up along an ornate shelf that went around the perimeter of the room. The shelf and her walls were painted a soft, pretty yellow and I gasped when I entered. It was unlike any room I'd seen. It was a tribute to horses. And, since Kelly didn't have any brothers or sisters to mess up her room, it had a perfection that my room, with its books on the floor and old desk, lacked.

I looked to Nicole to give her a "isn't this nice" look. She held a glass horse figurine she'd taken from Kelly's dresser. We smiled at each other.

Kelly put a record on the player in her room and we all spread onto her bed to listen to "Upside Down" by Diana Ross.

"Whoa. Who's that?" I asked.

"My mom listens to it and I just like it. She got me my own record" Kelly said.

Kelly showed us her closet too. It had plush, off-white carpet and clothes organized by type and color. Her long sleeve shirts hung by blues, browns, reds and greens, followed by short sleeve blouses, dresses and pants. Each of about ten boxes that lined the shelves above the hanging clothes had labels: *summer sandals*, *black patent leather* and *wellies*.

"My mom took me shopping in Boston and Nantucket this summer."

I guessed to myself Nantucket was in Massachusetts. I was very good at geography.

"My mom shops from the Saks Fifth Avenue catalogue," Melissa said. "She got me these jeans from there."

"I got mine at the mall," Lisa, said. "You can buy Calvin Klein anywhere."

I felt the now familiar rush of the foreign and the unknown wash over me just listening to them all talk about clothes. Even Nicole knew stuff they knew, and I felt really left out. I didn't know the first thing and my mom never got catalogues just for clothes in the mail. She got catalogues from seed company's and stained-glass manufacturers. So, I didn't have anything to say.

The rest of the party I looked at everybody's clothes in a totally new way. I counted seven horses on collared shirts, five looped pocket jeans and ten alligator shirts. When I overheard Will mention that he played the drums, I noticed he had a horse on his red shirt. On the way home I decided that the whales had to go.

Later I wrote in my diary:

Dear Diary,

Kelly's party was weird. We didn't do stuff like we normally do at birthday parties like run around and play and stuff, except when we did a sack race, which was really stupid. I felt like a grown up at her house. When I got home, I asked Mom if we could go shopping again because I wanted an alligator shirt and Mom got mad and yelled at me. I wonder if I'll ever look like the girls in my class. But I also wonder if I really want to? Can't I just be me?

5

The Saturday after Kelly's party Lisa's mom asked Mom and me to come over to their house for dessert. I thought it was really weird, but Mom was excited.

"She said she wanted to get to know us since Lisa talks about you. See, you're making new friends already. Plus, she made chocolate brownies."

I loved brownies and I liked Lisa, so I was excited, but I still thought it was weird to go to someone's house just for dessert on a school night. Nicole's mom never asked Mom to do that. They just talked at the softball practices and whenever they dropped one of us off somewhere or arranged a sleep over.

At Lisa's house, we sat around the table in their kitchen. They had a little nook with a long black and green cushion with beige pond scenes embroidered on the cushions. "They're precious," Mom complimented Mrs. Boswell.

"Thank you. I made them myself. Lisa and I take a knitting class together on Thursday nights and I'm teaching her to needlepoint."

I looked over at Lisa. She shrugged and smiled.

"Lisa tells us you're one of the smartest girls in your class," Mrs. Boswell said as she sipped her tea. She held her pinky up as she drank.

I didn't know what to say. I didn't think it was true and I couldn't believe Lisa would say that to her mom.

I stammered. Mom put her hand on my back and rubbed it the way I like. "We're very proud of her." She said.

"How is this different from your old school Molly?" Mrs. Boswell asked.

"Just different, I guess," I answered, not sure why I was getting grilled on this stuff again. "Ms. Byers is a really good teacher. I like her a lot."

"We're just so happy that Molly gets this opportunity and that the school system is taking notice of some of the more gifted children." My mom said to her.

Lisa yawned and Mrs. Boswell suggested she take me upstairs to show me her room.

"So, Mrs. Greeley and I can get acquainted."

I kinda felt sorry for Lisa. Her mom was so proper. She reminded me of Nelly's mom on the "Little House on the Prairie" – always concerned with appearances and scolding Nelly for doing things wrong. But I didn't want to say anything to Lisa. She probably loved her mom and was used to her.

As Lisa led me up a long wooden staircase that connected to the kitchen, Lisa told me they had two staircases that went up to the rooms upstairs, one was at the front of the house and we were taking the servant's stairs.

"But we don't have servants," Lisa told me as we climbed, "These are just left over from the olden days when people had them. We have a cleaning lady though, Agatha, but she's more like family to us. She comes over every day and takes care of us after school."

Seemed to me that all these new girls had upstairs at their houses. When we went upstairs at my house it meant we were coming up from the basement laundry room to the kitchen, not up higher than the ground.

At the top of the stairs was a long white hallway with a plush red rug with tiny yellow flowers all over it lining the walkway. Along the white walls were tons of photographs in different frames – some old some new.

"Who are all these people," I asked.

"Oh, that's just everybody. Like here's my great-great-great grandma." Lisa pointed to a really old wooden frame with a black and white photo in the cut-out center of board. The woman looked a little mean. Her hair all tied back in a bun and her collar so high on her neck. "She lived in this house too. So, did a lot of them. My mom inherited it from her mom."

I tried to imagine all these people living in the house. It gave me the creeps and I shook out a shiver.

Lisa's room was a lot bigger than mine. As I looked into it from the doorway, her bed seemed really far away against a wall. A big white rug was next to her bed. I thought it was a good idea because the hard wood floors were probably really cold at night. The walls were painted different shades of blue. One wall was all white, one a dark blue, another a light blue and another a medium blue. I liked it. And, along the white wall hanging over her bed was her name "LISA" written in big yellow pillow letters.

"That's neat," I said to Lisa.

"Thanks. My mom made it. She let me sew some of the letters though. See the "S"? I had some trouble with that one. You can see the stitching is crooked. But Mom said it was okay that I didn't do it perfect."

"Oh," was all I could say.

A big, old-looking dresser stood along the light blue wall. It had a huge mirror attached to it. The mirror was surrounded by wooden curls and flowers as decoration.

"Wow," I said. "I love that mirror."

"It was my grandma's. I love it too."

Two framed photographs sat on top of the dresser. One was of Lisa and her two sisters, Margaret and Karen. Lisa was in the middle, smiling; her sisters on either side of her looking very serious. I picked it up. They wore bathing suits.

"That's from Mackinac Island last summer. We were posing like models. And this one," Lisa said as she picked up the other photo, "is of me, Melissa and Kelly at last year's trip to the symphony. Our teacher took it."

The photo showed the three of them dressed in red and black dresses. Kelly's was plaid, Melissa's plain black and Lisa's plain red with a black belt. They were all smiling really big and looked like they were having fun when it was taken.

"You get to go to the symphony?"

"Yeah. Every year the whole school goes. It's usually really boring. We have fun on the bus though."

I wanted to tell Lisa I thought the symphony would be really fun. I'd always wanted to hear all those instruments, like the drums, the clarinet, the cello and all that played together. But Lisa didn't seem to like it, so I didn't say anything. I was a guest and my mom always said that a guest should be polite.

"Let's go to Karen's room." Lisa grabbed my hand and led me out the door.

"Won't she mind?" I asked enjoying Lisa's hand in mine. Were we officially friends now?

"They aren't home. They're at a play rehearsal. Besides, I don't care what they think. They treat me like a baby."

I thought back to the picture on Lisa's dresser. They looked like they liked each other.

"What's it like having big sisters?" I asked.

"It usually sucks. They tell me what to do and boss me around. And, sometimes they ignore me. They act so busy all the time."

I thought that I'd be a good big sister and never do that to my little sibling.

"But they have cooler stuff," she said when she opened one door. "This is Karen's room. Look at all her posters. I keep asking my mom if I can put up posters, but she says, "not until your older." Lisa mimicked her mom's voice in a nasally wine.

I looked around. Karen had a bigger bed than Lisa and her walls were all white and covered in posters of boys. Long, shiny posters of boys with blond hair, brown hair, black hair. I think some of them were in rock bands and some were actors. I didn't really know. But they smiled down on us as Lisa looked through underwear drawers and held up a white bra.

"Karen's a B-cup."

"Is that good," I asked.

"Duh. It's bigger than A."

"You've got to see something I found the other day," Lisa said. She led me to the bed and asked me to hold up the mattress while she reached underneath it.

"What were you doing?" I asked.

"You know. Hiding places."

She pulled out a magazine. It was called *Playgirl* and showed a guy, kinda like the ones on the wall, wearing a pair of unzipped blue jeans, a cowboy hat and no shirt. It looked like he was on a farm because he leaned against a stack of hay. Inside the magazine were pictures of men leaning against walls and washing their cars naked.

"Gross," I said and handed the magazine back to Lisa.

"I know, but just look," she showed me a picture of a guy touching his thing. He smiled at us.

I just had to laugh. "They're so nasty."

"You've got to read this," Lisa reached further under the mattress, grabbed a paperback book and threw it on my lap. Inside a bookmark with a red apple on it and a white fluffy top marked the page. I looked at the title: *Forever* by Judy Blume

"Sounds so dramatic," I said.

"Just read it." Lisa settled next to me on the bed and I read aloud:

We both left on our underpants but after a minute Michael was easing mine down and then his fingers began exploring me. I let my hands wander across his stomach and down his legs and finally I began to stroke Ralph.

"Who's Ralph?" I asked.

"You know. His thing." Lisa said. She grabbed the book and read on in a silly, exaggerated voice. *Oh yes … yes … yes.*

I tried to laugh with Lisa when she stopped, but I felt like I was pretending. I didn't think it was funny. It was too weird.

Even after I got home, when I went to bed that night, I couldn't stop thinking about Lisa rolling on her sister's bed saying "yes, yes, yes," the picture of the man in the magazine and Ralph. I felt funny, like a wet down in my private parts. Did I pee my pants? I went to the bathroom. I touched it. It felt cold, but I felt warm, so I was confused.

I wondered if Mike Spangler thought about stuff like this too.

The next Saturday afternoon I had the house all to myself. Mom was off running errands and Dad and Colin were at the ballpark having a father son outing. I walked around and noticed the silence, unsure how to use my time alone. I looked into the refrigerator and didn't find anything good. I looked again. I folded the clothes Mom left on my bed and put them away. I tried to read, but I didn't feel like it. I played the stereo.

Since Mom and Dad dominated the music playing in our house, I never got to play stuff I wanted to hear, like Diana Ross and disco. But I didn't even have any of those records – just the old records from when I was little, like a bunch of fairytales read out loud. I was bored with those now. Mom didn't understand that I wanted to have my own music around now. And, ever since Kelly played us a record on her very own stereo in her room, I wanted my own too.

I chose one of Mom's Linda Ronstadt albums and turned the volume up loud. I took the old tape recorder Dad gave around the house and interviewed some appliances and plants. I liked to interview stuff in the house and create stories and voices from the information I gathered.

On the way around the house, I sidestepped into my parent's room to rummage through Mom's drawers. I guessed I couldn't think Lisa was so wrong for looking through her sister's room, I did this all the time. It really was like searching for buried treasure. Sometimes I didn't find anything, and sometimes I'd find something interesting amongst her satin panties and hosiery. I guess everyone has their hiding places.

One time I found a pack of cigarettes wrapped inside a bra. And, another, I found a faded journal from when Mom was in college. She'd written about a dancing date with a guy named Dan. She liked him and I wondered what ever happened to him, but I was afraid I might get in trouble for snooping if I asked Mom about him. I wondered what it was like for her at my age. Did she like the boys in her class?

This time tucked under a bunch of silk scarves, I found a book called *The Joy of Sex*. I'd never seen it before. I flipped through the pages and saw outlines of men and women together on everyone. It made me think about Ralph in *Forever*.

As I investigated the pages, I noticed a tingling and throbbing between my legs. It felt strange, different and very good. I'd never felt that sensation before, but it was similar to one I felt when Lisa and I read the book at her house.

I put *The Joy of Sex* down as I heard the front door open. I felt a rush of fear through my body.

"Molly! We're home." Mom yelled in her sing-songy voice.

My hands shook as I covered the book in panties and closed the underwear drawer. I skipped out of my parent's room into my own right next to it and plopped onto the bottom bunk, grabbed my social studies book and pretended to read. My face gushed red. I sensed Mom at the door.

"Sweetie. What are you up to? The music is so loud."

"Nothing. Just homework."

Mom opened the bedroom door and I felt my face red hot.

"Honey, how can you study with this music on so loud?"

"Don't you know how to knock?" I said.

"Well, excuse me," Mom said and closed the door behind her.

I was confused. Why did the books make me feel so funny?

Later that night, I couldn't sleep. The pictures of those men and the throbbing between my legs stuck in my head. Where did that feeling come from, I wondered. I touched myself between my legs and felt the softness of my nightgown next to my skin.

The next day, I snuck back into my parents' room and stole the book from Mom's drawer. I hid it in my desk under all the old *Highlights* magazines.

At school on Monday, I felt special like I had a secret or $20 I could spend on anything I wanted. I skipped to my desk and even smiled at Will when I passed by him. I didn't think he saw me, but it felt good to me that I just did it. I knew and that was enough.

Ms. Byers wore a gold brooch on her white crocheted shawl and when the light from overhead hit it, shadows danced on the black board. Big excitement came when Jerry Johnson read the word of the day, *kaleidoscope*, then vomited all over Ms. Byers' desk. Some kids laughed. It made me feel sick. He had to go home early. Mr. Swenson, the janitor, put sawdust on the floor to get rid of the puke, but nothing got rid of the smell.

At recess, Nicole and I practiced our special tricks on the monkey bars. At our old school we had all sorts of routines that involved hanging upside down and pretending we were gymnasts. This new school had a completely different jungle gym, so we had to make up new routines. In-between a somersault over the bars, I asked Nicole if she'd ever touched herself between her legs.

"Gross. No way." She dangled upside down and held her skirt with one hand over her white tights as she dismounted.

"Why?" I held upside down and mimicked her dismount.

"Teddy told me you'd go to Hell."

An image of how Teddy might look naked popped into my mind. Once I walked in on Teddy when he didn't lock the bathroom door. I was so embarrassed because he was Nicole's brother and two years older than me.

"I don't believe in Hell." I looked Nicole in the eyes. "Besides, it can't be true. It feels so good."

Nicole stopped mid-climb up the rim of the bar and stared back at me.

"What? You mean you've done it?"

"Yeah." I did another somersault and dismount off the bars and landed in the sand.

"When?"

"Yesterday."

"Doesn't that mean you're not a virgin anymore?"

"I don't think so."

"Well, that's what Teddy told me."

Nicole walked away and left me alone at the bars. All of a sudden, my stomach hurt. Something between Nicole and me changed in that moment. I wondered, why didn't she ask me questions or even laugh? Why did she walk away? I thought she'd been mean to me and wished I didn't say anything to her. I'd wanted her to enjoy that good feeling too, but I didn't know how to tell her about it.

The recess bell rang, and we returned to Room 12. Nicole wouldn't look at me. And even though, I didn't think I'd done anything wrong – on the contrary, it felt so right – I felt bad. I regretted telling Nicole anything. But I was confused because she was supposed to be my very best friend.

The ride home from school was quiet. Nicole and I sat in the backseat as my mom told us about a weird guy she met at the deli counter at the supermarket. I barely listened. To me it felt like a thick shield of ice separated me and Nicole. I imagined writing in the ice with the tip of my forefinger *I hate you* in backwards letters so she could read it from her side of the backseat.

I didn't really understand why I hated her so much, but I also didn't know why she wouldn't talk to me.

The next day at school, no one talked to me. No one. Even when Ms. Byers asked me to stand in front of the class to read the day's word (*trachea, noun, the tube in air-breathing vertebrates that conducts air from the throat to the bronchi, strengthened by incomplete rings of cartilage. Also called windpipe.*) the entire class looked down towards their desk or out the window. I felt like I was standing alone in the midst of a vast desert – relief and water far from my sight. When I finished reading my entry, I looked to Ms. Byers for any indication of my existence. She nodded her head, smiled and winked at me. I went back to my seat confused.

Will and Bret chuckled as I walked past them at gym class, and I was the last to be picked for the stupid dodge ball game. Mark threw the ball in my direction and it hit me hard in the arm.

By the end of the day, it was clear that everyone knew something I didn't. Even the less popular kids ignored me. I felt like I didn't have a friend in the world. Ms. Byers asked me to talk to her after school.

"Is there anything the matter, dear?"

"I don't know."

"You seem quiet today. Sad."

A tear formed inside my eye and I felt like I had air stuck in my trachea. "I just don't understand."

"Understand what?"

I felt uncomfortable standing next to her. With my hands behind my back, I held onto my own hand. I noticed Ms. Byers' pretty brooch again. I shifted my weight in my shoes. Could I tell her? Was she safe?

"I don't understand why some people won't talk to me."

Ms. Byers put her hands on her lap. She smiled at me. I felt able to breathe again. "What gives you the idea someone's not talking to you?"

"They just aren't. I can tell."

"Sometimes it's not about anything you've done. Sometimes people are just caught up in their own needs. I'm sure it's nothing dear. Don't worry so much. Try not to be so hard on yourself."

"Dear Diary,

I've had a terrible day. Nobody talked to me at all except Ms. Byers and Mom. I have a feeling that Nicole told Melissa or somebody what I told her yesterday, but I don't know for sure. Maybe I'm just imagining things. But I thought we were the wacky twins and we could tell each other these things. Maybe it's like Ms. Byers said, it has nothing to do with me. But it's too weird. I feel like I want to talk to Nicole about it, but what if I'm just making it up? Maybe I should just not say anything. I don't know what to do. I do know that anything that feels good can't be bad. I do know that. Ice cream is good and it's not bad. Smiling feels good and it's not bad. So there. I better get started on my reading homework. We're reading The Cay. *Love Molly."*

Later that night I touched myself down there just to be sure once again that it was okay. When I'd reassured myself that I was happy doing it, I feel asleep.

The next day was a cold one. When I looked out the window from my bed, I saw white tips of frost on the front lawn. I grabbed a sweater from a short stack in a wicker basket at the foot of my bed. I kept all my winter clothes in that basket. I thought of the coming snowy season and shivered. I loved snow, but I didn't like being cold all the time. The winter before, Nicole and her brother took me sledding a few times and I wondered if we'd go again this year.

When Nicole and her mom picked me up for school, Nicole smiled large and said, "good morning," in her best imitation of Cowboy Bob, the local kid's television celebrity. We'd seen him in person when Mom took us to the pumpkin patch last year. He wore a huge cowboy hat. We thought he was funny and almost peed our pants when we laughed at our own imitations of his voice and the way he walked sideways on each foot, like he was dancing with a cow on its hind legs.

"Good morning," I repeated back to her in a most proper voice. Nicole gave me a one-eyed wink and smiled.

At school, Nicole grabbed my hand and encouraged me to skip with her up the flight of stairs to Room 12. We laughed as our feet squeaked on the hardwood floors. I almost slipped and Nicole kept me upright. We were jolly and I loved it. Maybe Ms. Byers was right, I thought, maybe yesterday was just a figment of my imagination. Maybe it had nothing to do with me. Life certainly seemed back to normal with me and Nicole.

We had our first fight ever in third grade. We played opposite day the whole day at school. We did this thing where one of us would say or do something and the other had to do the opposite. And, we'd do the opposite of what our teacher instructed, if only for a minute. We got big laughs, but I went too far at the water fountain one day. She was bent over taking sips of water and I shoved her out of the way to prove my turn was the opposite of hers. It was obnoxious, but that was the point of the whole game.

Nicole got really mad and the next day she told me she was mad and that I'd had hurt her feelings. I felt bad but I was glad she told me. We hugged and that was the end of that. We argued a few times since and we always told each other we were mad and why.

I figured all was well with Nicole and me; she'd tell me if she had anything to say to me.

During quiet reading time, she passed me a note.

Mike Spangler is so cute.

I smiled and wrote back

Ooh la la!

At recess, all us girls: Nicole, Kelly, Melissa, Lisa and I met up under the big evergreen on the playground. Shielded by the wind and bundled in our coats and mittens, we pretended there was a big fire roaring in the middle of our circle.

Melissa called this pow-wow at lunch when she announced in a whisper to all of us "It's time to talk about the boys" like it was her job or something.

She started the meeting with a flip of her long brown hair, and I wondered how she got it to look so perfect. My hair was straight as a board and I didn't think I'd ever be able to feather it like her. I didn't even know how to do it.

"Melissa, how do you make your hair look like that?" I asked. I pulled my knit cap closer over my own head.

"My mom does it for me in the morning with hot rollers. And, once a month I go to her hairdresser and she does it for me. When she does it, it lasts way longer."

"Do you use hair spray?" Nicole asked.

"Yah." Melissa smiled.

"My mom won't let me use it." Lisa said. She had really thin and curly, wispy hair.

"My Mom won't either," Kelly said. I was surprised since Kelly's mom let her listen to disco.

"Molly, will your mom let *you* use hair spray?" Melissa asked.

"I don't' know. I've never asked." I said. I'd never asked my mom anything about hair and stuff like that and she never mentioned it to me.

Melissa barely gave me a chance to think more on it because she practically interrupted me to say "Let's get to business. And the topic today is boys. Who likes who?" She looked at each of us. "Who wants to start?" She clapped her hands together.

I bet she was really good at playing teacher. I thought. And, then I panicked. I felt my face grow hot and dry. I didn't want to be called. I didn't know what to say since this pow-wow was so spur of the moment. I didn't have time to think.

"I like Mark," Melissa said. She crossed her ankles in front of her again, right into our mock fire.

"Hey, that's our fire," Lisa said.

"Who do you like?" Kelly asked her.

"I don't know." I figured Lisa would know. She knew all about Ralph. I watched as she zipped her jacket further up for warmth – it looked almost exactly like Kelly's only hers was blue and Lisa's was green.

"You don't know?" Melissa asked. She laughed and flipped her hair again. "Well, think hard and we'll come back to you."

I wondered if Nicole was going to say Mike Spangler. We all knew he was the cutest in our class. But he was also really quiet, and it was hard to know anything about him. I hadn't heard him laugh yet and I wondered how Nicole would react if someone said his name before her. I thought he was cute, but I didn't know if I *liked him* liked him.

"I guess I like Jerry Johnson." Lisa said.

"What?" Melissa and Kelly said together. They giggled.

"He just puked in front of the whole class," Nicole said. I flicked Nicole's arm with my fingers. That was mean of them, I thought.

"I think you were out sick that day, Lisa," I said and smiled at her.

"I like, um, Brian Stevens."

"But he's a sixth grader," Melissa said. "You can't like a sixth grader. It has to be someone in our class. Think some more. There has to be someone."

Wow, I thought. I should see if she wants to play school sometime.

"What about you Nicole," Lisa asked.

"That's easy," Melissa said. "She likes Mike Spangler."

"How do you know?" Nicole patted her hands onto her skirt and smiled with her chin down.

"Come on. You stare at him all day. And you always try to stand near him in line."

I watched Nicole's smile curl onto her face. Her cheeks turned red. "Yah." She giggled. "He's so cute." And then a high-pitched squeak came flying out of her mouth.

I laughed. Melissa shot me a look. "What about you Molly? Who do you stare at?"

I was nervous. I warmed my hands on the mock fire and just blurted "Will." I wanted to say it with as much confidence as Melissa, even Nicole, but it didn't sound like them. After I said it, I felt my hands shaking. I didn't want to be made fun of, and no one said anything. Melissa turned to Kelly since she still hadn't answered.

"I thought I was safe since you all know I've liked Bret since second grade."

"Our new girls don't know that," Melissa said and pointed to me and Nicole.

Lisa interrupted Melissa's point to say, "I'll take Kevin. He's way cuter than Jerry Johnson."

"Good choice," Melissa said.

Everyone was pretty quiet for a while.

"Now what," I asked the group.

"Now we wait. Now we know." Melissa answered.

The bell rang and we wiped our backsides free of cold dirt and skipped inside. I felt, for the first time since being at the new school, like I was included. I felt good.

6

That next Saturday Mom and Papa threw a birthday party for Colin at Showbiz Pizza Palace. Dad really wanted to be there, but he had a lot of work to do, so, it was just the four of us and two of Colin's friends.

The place was crazy with flashing lights, way too bright colors and the clangs and bangs of video games and pinball machines. Kids screamed and ran around like wild hyenas while their parents sat with lazy grins. We ordered a large pizza with pepperoni and pitchers of Pepsi. Presents, one wrapped in the Sunday comics, lay on the table, but Colin wasn't interested in them. He and his friends were so excited about all the video games and plastic prizes they could buy by accumulating tickets when they scored high. The higher the score, the more tickets you got.

I loved video games, but each time I walked past my favorite games, Centipede and Space Invaders, they were occupied; so, I played skeet ball instead. I threw the heavy brown ball up the tower of rings and tried to get it into the littlest hole at the top. I was pretty good and won enough tickets to get Colin a package of plastic Army guys.

The prize booth was lit up like a parade float and covered top to bottom with stuffed animals. A large mechanical furry contraption was right next to it. So, after I bought the Army guys, we checked it out. It was a life-size replica of Billy Bob, Showbiz's main character from the stage performance they gave every half hour on the hour with a keyboard on his chest. Two boys about my height had their backs to me and typed in words that Billy Bob repeated in a synthesized voice. Each word sounded like a high-pitched record played backwards by a robot.

"Billy Bob will not say that word." Billy Bob said.

"Try this," one of the boys said.

"Billy Bob says turd," the bear said. The boys laughed. The shorter one slapped his hand onto the keyboard.

"Dude," he said, elongating the "u" like he was a surfer.

"Let me try," said the taller one.

"Billy Bob will not say that word." The boys laughed again.

I watched and wondered what they asked it to say, then asked if I could play too. When the boys turned around to answer my question, it was Kevin and Mark. They were there for Mark's little brother's birthday party. Mark was the middle of two boys.

"Hey Molly." Kevin said. He smiled and stepped aside. "Go ahead." I typed in the word "poop'. "Billy Bob says poop."

"Neat," I said and laughed out loud. Kevin and Mark laughed too.

"I want him to say a real cuss word," Kevin said.

"Try fuck," Mark said and typed it in.

Billy Bob wouldn't say it. But we spent the next twenty minutes trying to get him to say words like ass, butt, tit, lick, and pee-pee. I had so much fun I forgot I was there for Colin's party. I forgot the Army toys in my pocket, and I forgot that Melissa liked Mark and Lisa liked Kevin. I was just being myself.

I told them I had to go and realized how strange it was to see them out of school without other kids around them. Playing with them was just like playing with Nicole sometimes, we just used different words and I let the boys do most of the typing since they'd started the game.

At the birthday table, Mom and Papa cleaned up pizza plates.

"We saved you a slice," Mom said.

"Where'd you run off to," Papa asked when I sat onto his lap.

"I saw some boys from school," I felt my face turn red and I didn't want to tell him we'd been trying to get Billy Bob to say bad words.

"We're having cake soon. Stay here if you want or come back in a few minutes," Mom said. "What boys?" She asked as an afterthought.

"Oh, just some kids from my school."

"How nice. I'm glad you have so many nice friends." And then patted me on the head like I was three. Sometimes she bugged me.

I stayed and ate my slice of cheese pizza. Later, Colin blew out his candles on the racecar-shaped ice cream cake from the Baskin Robins. We ate too much. I got a stomach ache and Colin puked on the way home. Papa had to carry him from the car to his bed.

The next day I called Nicole to tell her about seeing Kevin and Mark at Showbiz.

"And, you just played the game with them? That's it?" She asked.

"Yeah. Nothing else."

"I wonder if they like you?"

"I don't know. We just played with Billy Bob. I'll probably never talk to them again."

"Why? Maybe one of them wants to go with you."

The thought of that scared me so much, I couldn't tell Nicole.

"I don't like either of them. Besides, what's up with this going with thing anyways?" I truly did not understand how it worked.

"You know. A boy likes you and you like him back, so you go with each other."

"I know that. I mean, how does it start?" I couldn't imagine it ever happening to me.

"I don't know."

Nicole didn't know any more than me, but she said she'd ask her brother.

Melissa got in trouble by Ms. Byers for passing a note to Nicole during our Social Studies lesson. Ms. Byers made it a point to stop the lesson and her voice was impatient, flustered then calm as she told them they had better put the note away or she was going to read it in front of the whole class. I'd seen our music teacher do that before and I thought I'd just die if I got caught passing a note. I wondered what it said.

At recess, while a bunch of us played tag and ran around like Indians whopping air into our cupped and gloved hands, Bret smiled a lot at Kelly. She smiled back. I noticed that Nicole liked to run really close to Mike and he'd bump into her. Melissa and Mark held hands for a brief moment and Lisa and Kevin acted like they hated each other. Kevin tried to punch her in the arm but missed. Then Lisa walked away from him and folded her arms across her chest. Will ran and laughed and I just felt like I was on the outside watching a big group of monkeys play.

When I got home, I wrote about it:

Dear Diary,

I just don't understand this going with thing. What does it mean to go with someone? If the boy is supposed to start it, will one start it with me? Do I need hair spray? Maybe I'll ask Mom. Love, Molly

While Mom washed the dinner dishes, I asked her if she'd buy me hair spray. She looked down at me, over her big belly, dishtowel flung on her shoulder.

"Sweetie, that's stuff we can talk about when you're older, like Junior High. Girls your age don't need hair spray."

"But my hair won't curl." I took a crusty piece of noodle from a plate and flicked it into the soapy sink.

"It's not supposed to. You have straight hair."

"But everyone else has long, curly hair."

Mom huffed. "Surely, not everyone."

I decided to ask her about boys instead.

"What if a boy asked me to go with him? What would you say?"

"Who asked you that?" she said with a rush in her voice.

"Nobody." I didn't want to tell her about Will. "But all the girls want to go with boys. They talk about it all the time."

"Who's everyone? I don't like the sound of this."

I didn't want to tell on Nicole and Lisa. I knew their moms would find out if I told my mom. "Like Melissa and Kelly. They've already had boyfriends. And, Melissa wears a bra."

Mom grabbed bowls for ice cream and opened the freezer. I saw a carton of mint chocolate chip from the corner of my eye. It was my favorite. Mom was quiet for a few minutes and I let her think. Maybe she was going to tell me how it all worked. "I just think you're too young. Kids at your age don't need to be messing with this stuff. You should be studying. Maybe when you're in Junior High."

"You always say that."

"I just think that's when it should be. No sooner. We'll talk more later, but I don't want you to worry so much about what other people are doing."

I said okay, but inside I knew that every day it was harder and harder not to care what other kids did, what they wore and how they acted. I didn't want to be on the outside. I wanted in. But I didn't know how to get there.

7

One day we came back from recess and Ms. Byers had arranged the desks in Room 12 differently. We now had to sit in groups of four. Our names, written on folded construction paper meant to look like a tent on top of our desks, weren't in alphabetical order anymore. Ms. Byers announced in her sing-songy voice that these would be our new seats and groups as we planned and finished our oral reports. I was nervous and excited that my group had Kristi, Melissa, and Mark.

A boy named Adam read the word of the day (*extemporize, vti, to perform or speak without having made any preparation*) while he blew his nose into a white handkerchief. Then, Ms. Byers addressed the class. "Put on your creativity hats. Write down a list of animals you'd like to do a visual and oral report on. No two people can do the same one, so think beyond the ordinary."

I used my yellow notebook for my list. Nicole coughed and I looked over at her group which had Mike Spangler, Adam and Kelly. She looked around the room, her pencil in her mouth, thinking. I smiled at her and she smiled back.

"So, what do you guys think?" I asked my group. "I want to do my report on butterflies. What about you Melissa," I wrote *butterflies* on my page.

"How about horses? No, Kelly will probably pick that. I want to do it on turtles."

"Turtles are neat." I said.

"Melissa, you should write yours about poodles so you can talk about your mom's dog's visits to the hairdresser. That's creative." Mark said in his mock voice of Ms. Byers. I watched him scribble *fish* onto his paper. I raised my hand to ask Ms. Byers how many we should list.

"Class," Ms. Byers clapped her hands to get everyone's attention. "Molly just asked how many topics you should have on your list. Just think of as many as you can. What would you like to learn about? Since no two people can do the same topic, I suggest you come up with at least five."

As the room filled with our chatter, I struggled to think of anything besides butterflies. I loved them and I loved the idea that I could learn more about them for school. So, I decided to list only butterflies because I couldn't imagine anyone else would pick it.

Lisa sat directly behind me with Jerry Johnson, Bret and Jane. She passed me a note. I was scared I'd get caught reading it, but when I felt the weight of the paper folded four times, a rush of heat ran through my stomach and I carefully un-folded it.

Will wants to go with you.

I thought about this for a minute. How did Lisa have this conversation with Will? She did live across the street from him and they did walk to school together. Will made me smile. I liked his laugh. I was excited he liked me. Maybe this was what I'd been waiting for, I thought, someone to do something for me to react to. I was scared of what would happen if I answered *okay*.

I didn't want to give my answer to Lisa right away. I wanted to think about it. Or even just talk to Nicole after school. Besides I didn't want Ms. Byers to catch us. So, I put the note in the front pocket of my denim overalls jumper. Then, just as I focused on my group again, Lisa slipped me another one.

I held it under my desk and unwrapped it right away.

Do you want to go with him? Yes, No or Maybe. Circle one.

I looked around the room and watched Will as he read his list to his group. He wasn't the most popular boy, or the cutest, but he was nice, and I really liked him. Plus, Lisa was going with Kevin and Melissa was going with Mark. Bret and Kelly. Almost Nicole and Mike. I wanted to go with someone too.

"What about monkeys," said Mark. "I want to find out why they have big red butts." Melissa and Kristi giggled. I quickly circled "Yes." I checked for Ms. Byers, who was across the room and passed the note back to Lisa.

I wasn't sure what was supposed to happen next. Would Will come talk to me at lunch or should I approach him? Since this was my first time in this situation, I had questions and nerves. I bit my nails.

Nicole giggled with Mike and Kelly. I really wanted to talk to her about it. But, at lunch I didn't get a chance because she sat in-between Melissa and Lisa and I sat next to Kelly at the end of the lunch table. Kelly talked the whole time about her plans for Christmas break. It seemed ages away to me. Will sat at the table behind us and didn't even look at me. I was confused and decided to talk to Lisa.

I caught up to her at recess as she was doing tricks on the monkey bars with Melissa. I noticed they wore the same red shoes. They did some moves they learned in gymnastics class together. I thought the tricks Nicole and I did were better. I looked around for Nicole, but I didn't see her.

They stopped in mid-trick with their legs on the bars and heads upside down. Their long hair dangled in the air. I wondered if Melissa had ultra-strength hairspray because her hair held in big clumps around her ears like feathers on a duck.

"Hey Molly. What's up?" Lisa asked as she jumped from her position and landed on her feet in the sand.

"I was just wondering what happened with that note I sent you."

"Oh, the note," Lisa said. She looked over her shoulder to Melissa. Melissa finished her trick and stood behind Lisa and was soon joined by Nicole and Kelly. They seemed to show up from nowhere.

"That was just a joke Molly." Lisa looked to Melissa again and smiled.

I looked at Nicole and she looked down at the ground. Kelly giggled under her breath.

"What do you mean?" I asked. My stomach rolled into knots.

"We just wanted to see if you'd say yes in case, he, or anyone ever, which they won't, asks you to go with them," Melissa said.

I tried to hold back tears that just automatically came into my eyes and blurted "Well that was pretty pathetic Lisa."

Their faces and bodies became blurry. I felt the sting of tears in my eyes. In silence, I turned and, in a daze, walked slowly towards the back door of the school. Still in my haze, I asked Ms. Garth if I could use the bathroom. I went into the toilet stall, closed the door and stared at the holes in the ceiling panels. I counted 347 before the end of recess bell rang. I tried to erase the memory of the playground from my mind, like erasing chalk from the blackboard. But it didn't work.

We chose our talk topics that afternoon and I sat at our table with my fists clenched under my desk. It took every ounce of control I had not to throw my social studies book across the room. I imagined the sound the window glass would make as it shattered on the floor.

"Okay. Let's go around in alphabetical order and you can all choose your topic," Ms. Byers announced.

I thought for one second that it would be a small ounce of happiness in my horrible day when I got to say *butterflies* and imagined one landed on my arm.

"Jane Buckley," Ms. Byers called.

"Butterflies," I heard Jane answer.

I felt my body slip into my chair. I hadn't even written anything else because I was so sure butterflies were mine.

When it was my turn, I was stumped. I blurted "snakes" after I saw one on a nature book on the shelf next to my desk.

After class I went to speak with Ms. Byers aware only that I didn't see any way I wanted to do a report on snakes. While she straightened the papers on her already super neat desk, I asked her if I could do butterflies instead. She said no without even looking up at me. I told her I really didn't like snakes and suggested maybe Jane and I could both do different kinds of butterflies; like maybe she could do North America and I could do Europe or something. Ms. Byers looked up, gave me a sweet smile that shot ounces of honey through my body, but her answer was still no.

"Fair is fair," she said.

Once we picked, that was it.

"Remember to look at snakes not with fear, but fascination," she said. "They are creatures of many talents and I'm sure you will learn much from them."

I thanked her and felt heavy as I walked out of school.

Nicole was in the car, excited about her topic. Her mom listened with rapt attention. She wore her nurses' uniform and I noticed her nametag missed a letter of her name. Instead of Claudia it said Claudi. For some strange reason seeing her nametag gave me the honey feeling again. And, I put on my nice self for the ride home.

"What did you choose again Nicole? I forgot." I asked. I placed my book bag on my lap.

"Dogs."

"That's neat. You can interview Barney," I said while I watched the big houses go by the car.

Nicole and her mom laughed. Their golden retriever Barney was the envy of the whole neighborhood. He was vivacious, loving and so much fun to be with. I was jealous she chose so easily and got to do her report on something she knew about. I guess I didn't mind that I had to do extra work and reading; but I really wanted to get butterflies.

Nicole didn't mention what happened on the playground during recess. I didn't know what to say about it, so I kept my mouth closed on the way home.

I wrote in my diary in bed with a flashlight on my lap:

> *Dear Diary,*
>
> *I am so sad. I feel funny like I got hit by a bike going too fast or swallowed too much water in the pool. First. I don't understand all this going together stuff and how it works. Is there something wrong with me? I can't help feeling like everyone knows something that I don't. And, with the note and everything and how mean Melissa, Kelly, Nicole and Lisa were at recess. Why did they do that? I'm scared to say anything. I just want everything to go back to normal with us all being friends and stuff.*
>
> *Also, does Will really like me or not? I don't think so, but if he does, what do I do?*
>
> *I can't talk to Nicole now. I'm too mad at her. Plus, she got dogs and I got snakes. Molly*

Later that night, I felt between my legs again. I still liked it. Again, I wondered: if it felt good and what happened at school that day felt bad, then it couldn't be so bad after all. But I wasn't going to tell anyone about it.

8

I sat on my bed reading my snake book, *Venomous Reptiles of North America*. I couldn't concentrate though. Mom blabbed on the phone in their bedroom next to mine and she was so loud.

I noticed the butterfly posters on my walls. Papa taught me about their scientific order, and I liked to think of him when I read, *Lepidoptera,* written in a fluffy cursive on the bottom of the white borders. I liked how the "p" and "t" were next to each other. I didn't usually encounter too many words that did that.

I thought for a moment that I never got what I wanted. It was a new thought brought on by wondering why I didn't get to write my report on butterflies. Why did stupid Jane get butterflies instead of me?

My closet door was ajar and for the first time I was surprised by how small and dingy my closet seemed now that I'd been to Kelly's house. Where Kelly had carpet in her closet, I had wood floors; Kelly had matching wooden hangers, mine were a mish mash of white plastic hangers that came with new clothes and ancient, musty wooden hangers from Grandma's closet. I imaged they had once hung the fox wraps and the two-piece wool skirt suits Mom took to Goodwill after she died. Now they held hand-me downs from my cousin Sheila. Kelly's closet was quadruple the size of mine and, of course, had all brand-new, designer clothes. Kelly's little sister could easily play inside it, for hours at a time, and not get claustrophobic. Hers even had a light inside.

I was startled by a knock on the door and my book fell from my lap onto the floor.

"Yah?" I heard myself say. My palms were moist.

"Can I come in, sweetie?" Mom's voice was soft.

She carried a book and sat at the foot of my bed. With the book on her lap, she said, "I'd like to talk to you for a minute about sex."

My heart skipped a beat and it seemed like the room froze.

"Uh, sure."

She adjusted her weight on bed. I watched for her face to grow red. Was she nervous I wondered. "I bought you this book. I thought you might like it."

She handed me *What's Happening to My Body: A Growing Up Book for Girls.*

I said "thanks," and prepared myself for the inevitable.

My mouth went dry as I flipped through the book – my stomach went to the butterflies. I felt an odd combination of eww gross and an urge to see if there were pages with the naked pictures. I wondered if there were photos of people doing it. My belly tightened again. I was embarrassed to talk to Mom about sex. I felt like I knew something she didn't, and I couldn't tell her about it. No way.

Mom shifted on the bed and smoothed her palms over her thighs. She watched as I flipped through the book.

"Do you have any questions," she asked.

"Not really," I said even though I wanted to ask if it was wrong to touch yourself down there. I just couldn't ask it. I was afraid the same way I got afraid to get out of bed at night when the light wasn't on – it was like I couldn't move.

"Well, then. Let me know if and when you do. I hope you like the book. Maybe it will help you think of some questions."

She put her fingernails through my hair, gave me a big squeeze and stepped out and closed my door. I settled onto my pillow unsure of what just happened.

When I went to bed that night, I flipped through the book and wondered about Will again. And Ralph. If girls and boys are meant to be together for sex and other things, how does it start? I wondered how you even got in a conversation with a boy that would lead to taking your clothes off. I knew I wasn't ready for that. But I just wondered.

A week after Mom gave me the sex book, there was serious drama at school. Melissa stopped talking to Mark and she made sure everyone knew about it. She walked in a huge L around him every time she had to be near him. She talked real loud about him at lunch. By this time, all of us girls, me, Nicole, Lisa, Melissa and Kelly always sat together at lunch. Nobody mentioned what happened at recess that one day, so I just tried to forget about it too. And, although we ate together every day, I wasn't sure if I totally trusted any of them. I wanted friends and they kept inviting me to be in the group, so, I joined. It just became natural to hang out with them.

For a whole week, Melissa said mean things about Mark at lunch and it was always loud enough so he could hear.

"Mark likes to play in the sandbox with dolls," she said on Monday.

"He's smelly jelly." She said on Tuesday and we all laughed.

Every day she said a new insult and Mark wasn't phased. He ignored her too. At the end of the week, Melissa announced she liked Bret. Kelly got totally upset and went home early with a stomach ache.

According to my sex book, boys and girls are totally different. And, I came to see it was true in every way imaginable. By the next week, Melissa and Mark were going together again, and I couldn't figure out what that meant.

9

I jumped rope on the sidewalk, practicing my moves, and even though the air was crisp, I was hot inside the sweater Mom said I should wear. I was all sticky and sweaty and took a break to watch the yellow, red and orange leaves rustle in the wind and fall to the ground. Then the mailman delivered a pink envelope with my name on it. I ripped it open and pulled out a heavy pink card.

You're Invited!
What: Melissa's Birthday Slumber Party!
Where: Melissa's house, 6430 Slaven Avenue
When: 6 p.m., Saturday, Oct. 27

In handwritten script at the bottom someone wrote the note:
Please bring a sleeping bag, pillow and other overnight necessities.

I ran into the kitchen. Mom washed the lunch dishes and was signing along to a Carpenter's song on the radio. "I'm on the top of the world looking down on creation."

"Mommy, Mommy, I just got invited to a slumber party."

"You did?" She dried her hands on the towel and draped it over her shoulder. "Let's see it?"

I re-read it over her shoulder. I was so excited. I'd never been to a real slumber party before – like the kind where a bunch of girls spend the night. It had only been Nicole and me at our sleepovers.

"I need to bring a sleeping bag, but I don't have one."

"Just use one of your Dad's Army bags. There are a few in the basement."

I thought of spiders and cobwebs and stomped onto the linoleum. "It's not fair. It'll be all buggy."

"Before you get hysterical, let's have a look. He just used one a month ago when he went to Ft. Bragg, so I'd imagine its ship shape."

We retrieved the sleeping bag and I knew right away that I would have trouble sleeping in it. It smelled musty, like it had been downstairs wrapped in plastic, rained on, and left to dry in a dark room full of wet moss.

I didn't want to take it to Melissa's. I couldn't.

Mom unrolled it onto the living room carpet.

"I saw a spider," I said and shook all over.

"We'll let it hang outside to air out. The spider will have to move on."

"No. I can't use it. I won't be able to sleep or stop thinking about it."

"There's another one downstairs."

"No." I stomped my feet again. "Don't you see? These are smelly and scary. I can't sleep in them."

"What will you sleep in then?"

"Can't we just go to the store so I can get my own sleeping bag?"

"No."

Mom carried the bag to the back door and gave it a rolling shake into the backyard. I followed her.

"Why not?"

"Because." She wouldn't look at me.

"Because why?"

She threw the bag over her shoulder and walked towards my room. I followed her. She didn't answer me. I could tell she was mad. But so was I.

"Because why?"

Mom leaned into me and spoke in a whisper between pursed lips, "Because we can't spend the money right now, that's why."

"This sucks." I jumped onto my bed. I just couldn't possibly go to the party knowing the other girls would have their own bags and ones that weren't their dad's smelly Army bags. I just couldn't. But it didn't matter what I thought. I never got what I wanted.

Since, in my opinion, Melissa was the scariest girl in our class, I wanted to get her a gift that she would really like. I called Nicole for ideas. I wanted to bring her something she would really like not because I cared for her or anything, but because I hoped it make it easier on me at school. I didn't want her to lash out at me at lunch just because she didn't like the present I gave her or because she thought it was too baby or something. That's what she'd said about an outfit Jane wore to school just after Kelly, Lisa and Nicole and I got the invitation to Melissa's party. She said to all of us, about Jane's outfit "it's so baby." And, Jane didn't get invited to the party. I didn't want to be Jane.

"I don't know," Nicole said. "Maybe some barrettes or something."

I thought barrettes would be good. Maybe if Melissa wore them, she wouldn't swing her hair around so much. But I couldn't get the same present as Nicole. Birthday presents aren't the same as shoes or jackets. You can't have the same. It has to be creative.

"Great idea. Maybe I'll get her some nail polish. I saw some with sparkles in it at the drugstore."

"That's perfect!"

I was glad to have a friend like Nicole that I could just call to help me think of good birthday presents. But I sensed something weird about our talk.

Dear Diary,

I'm nervous and excited about my very first slumber party at Melissa's. I'm happy she invited me because it proves that we are friends. I talked to Nicole about what to get her. She knows better than me. We hung up after only a few minutes. We used to talk forever and talk about stuff. But she didn't even sound excited or happy to hear me. She seemed tired and far away. She has these moods lately. It's annoying. Oh, and I'm annoyed that I can't get a sleeping bag of my own.

I think I'm getting Melissa a plethora (I learned that one at school this week) of nail polish for a present. Maybe we can paint each other's nails at the party.

Well, I gotta get my homework done. Smooches (If I don't who will?) Molly

By Saturday, I knew that I'd have to bring Dad's Army sleeping bag and I was not happy about it at all. I'd just be cool though. I thought. That was my plan. I had my Lucy pillowcase (my overnight necessity) and my favorite pjs– one of Dad's super soft old t-shirts and my favorite white flannel pants with little hearts all over.

At Melissa's, Kelly and Nicole sat huddled in the kitchen nook. Their sleeping bags, duffels, pillows and gifts piled around them and crowded the area, so I had to stand. I put my sleeping bag on the pile and waited for someone to make fun of it, but no one said a word. We hung around the kitchen until Lisa arrived.

"Let's go downstairs," Melissa said, and we followed her with our gear.

We passed a large living room decorated all in yellow. There was a lush yellow carpet, spotless yellow sofa and matching yellow armchairs surrounding a sparkling dark wood coffee table with a crystal vase filled with red roses. I felt suffocated just looking at the room.

"How pretty," Nicole said, her head part way in the room.

"Yeah, my mom had it decorated by Laura Ashley. We're not allowed in there. It's only for show."

I didn't know who Laura Ashley was, but I decided not to ask.

Two identical sectional couches, a game table, huge television and boxes of video games filled the basement room. Melissa's younger brothers played with the Colecovision on the floor.

"Get out," Melissa said. She put her arms on her hips.

"Hold on. We're not done yet," said the smallest one. He didn't look at her.

"Mom! Randy and Jason won't go upstairs!" Melissa made fists and stood over her brothers, "Get out. Or I'll kill you." She told them.

They left the video game running.

While we settled in and put our gifts on the coffee table. I'd never been in a basement that had carpet and wondered how all the stuff in her basement stayed dry when the rains came. Ours usually flooded.

Melissa's mom carried down a tray of nachos, popcorn and potato chips.

"Girls. Help yourselves. There's soda in the mini-fridge." She said pointing to a small refrigerator built into a book-filled wall unit. "Regular, diet and TAB."

Lisa dug into the glass bowl with "popcorn" in stenciled red letters around it. She put a mouthful in her hand and ate the popped corn in twos. I put a handful into one of the smaller bowls, identical to the big one, and took it to the couch. Kelly picked at each kernel, moving them around in her bowl. Was she looking for a good one, I wondered? They all looked the same to me. I loved the little bowls and matching big bowl. They were so wonderful – almost magical in their perfection. We had matching bowls at home, but they were just our regular bowls for cereal and spaghetti, not special ones just for popcorn.

"We have movies to watch," Melissa said. She jumped onto the couch and sat squat in front of Kelly. "She showed me how to work the Betamax and everything."

"What's a Betamax," I asked.

"Duh, it's the machine that plays tapes so you can watch movies on your TV anytime you want."

"See," Melissa said as she fanned out some tapes on the table "We have Star Wars."

I couldn't believe she had Star Wars at her house. Just last year I waited in line with my parents and Colin for two hours just to get into the movie theater. Melissa could watch it whenever she wanted.

"I love Star Wars," Nicole said. "Let's watch that."

"They're for later. Now we have games." Melissa unfolded a long piece of yellow lined paper and read from a list. "My mom organized it all. First, we're going to play Piggly-Wiggly because it's supposed to help us get our sleeping area together. Then we'll do a talent show or open presents and then we have Pizza for later and movies."

"What's Piggly-Wiggly," Nicole asked. "I never heard of it."

"It's fun. We played it at my cousin's house over the summer. Before we start, we have to set up our sleeping bags because they're a big part of the game. See." Melissa unrolled her baby blue bag in the middle of the carpet. "Everyone lays out their bags. Then we choose someone to be it. I can be it the first time to show you how we play. Then, since I'm it I have to leave the room and you have to all hide in a bag that isn't yours. I have to pick a bag and try to figure out who's inside. It's easy."

I immediately felt butterflies in my belly. I didn't want anyone in my bag.

Nicole put her pink bag next to Melissa's and Kelly laid her horse-covered bag on the other side of Melissa. Lisa hurried to put hers, which looked exactly like Melissa's, next to Nicole so I put mine next to Kelly. It was all a weird, fast dance that felt very competitive. I looked at the row of bags and mine totally stood out like a sore thumb. I felt embarrassed, but I tried to hide it because I just wanted to have fun.

"Let's start," I blurted. Just wanting to get it over with.

"Molly," Melissa says, pointing at my bag, "where'd you get your bag? The Salvation Army?"

The girls all laugh.

"Funny," I say back. "It's my dad's." I try to sound chipper, as my grandpa would say. "He let me use it. It's really cozy."

Melissa pokes at it with her finger. "It smells weird."

"That's just the Army smell. A lot of Army stuff smells like that. It's not bad."

"Is your dad in the Army or something?" Kelly asks. "What does he do?"

"Mostly he just goes on weekends sometimes and jumps out of airplanes. I don't know really."

Lisa interrupts my thoughts. "Do we have to play this stupid sleeping bag game? We did it last time and we're ten now. Besides, I brought these from my sisters."

Lisa throws a handful of *Tiger Beat* magazines onto the sleeping bags. We each grab one. I pick one with Willie Ames on the cover. He's on *Eight is Enough* – one of my favorite shows about a family with eight kids. He plays the second oldest brother, Tommy, and I like that he's always so nice to his little brother Nicolas.

"Scott Baio is such a fox," Lisa says holding up her magazine. I recognize him from one of the posters in her sister's room. Lisa flips through the magazine to show us a small foldout poster of him. He's wearing a bandana tied around his forehead and a sleeveless red t-shirt. It looks like he cut the sleeves off himself because you can see little strings hanging off one of them.

I flip through my magazine and come across a similar foldout poster. This one has Ricky Shroeder on it. He's blond and on a show called *Silver Spoons* where he plays a rich kid who has an obnoxious neighbor. "He's cute," I say, showing the poster around to the rest of the girls.

"He's kinda baby," Melissa says.

I start to feel like Melissa is on one of her mean missions again and excuse myself to go to the bathroom just as Melissa asks Kelly if she likes Adam. "I heard he wants to go with you," I hear her say. Does he really, I think? Isn't Kelly going with Shane? I'm so tired of talking about boys. It's kinda boring. Besides, no boy seems interested in me and I won't tell them a real person I like again since the last time I did they were so mean.

"Upstairs, first door on your right." Melissa tells me with a flip of her hand, barely looking at me.

I close the bathroom door behind me. The wallpaper is like old black and white newsprint from the days when women wore long dresses with high collars and men rode around the city on enormous bicycles – the kind where the front wheel is 100 times larger than the back. I touch the wall. It doesn't feel thin like regular newspaper paper – it's glossy and slick like dried glue.

I look in the mirror over the sink. My green eyes and all my freckles dominate my reflection. "So ugly," I think. "Nobody will ever want to go with me."

I feel so different from all of them. They are all so much prettier than me. They are the girls boys like. I don't understand why I'm even friends with any of them besides Nicole. I don't know what I'd do without her. I want the slumber party to bring us closer together.

I pick up an unlit candle from over the toilet and smell its vanilla fragrance, then wash my hands and dry them with the hand towel from the rack. They are much softer than the ones at home. Ours are harsh and have a few holes.

As I walk down the stairs, I hear Melissa and Nicole giggle.

"Duh. You can too pierce your ear with a needle and an ice cube. My sister did it to her friend and I watched," Lisa says.

"Hey, let's do a talent contest. We can all lip sync and do dances," Melissa says.

"Here. We can use my hairbrush as the microphone," Nicole says.

"I don't know what to sing," Lisa says, her legs arched under her chin.

Melissa dumps an entire box of tape cassettes on the carpet.

"Wow," Kelly says.

I agree. We only have a few at home. My parents still haven't gotten me a boom box or an allowance to buy tapes.

"My mom has a ton of Linda Ronstadt," I say.

"Who's that?" Melissa says.

"My mom's favorite singer. She's good."

"Any music your mom listens to is usually old stuff," Nicole says.

"Not my mom," Kelly says. "She likes Diana Ross."

I feel like saying, "Duh, we know Kelly." But I don't. I want to have fun, not be mean.

Melissa opens a cupboard under their huge television console and pulls out a brand-new music player. It still has a sticker over the tape cassette holder. She peels it off. "I'm gonna sing The Jackson Five. "ABC"!"

I don't know what to sing. I don't listen to my own music – just stuff I hear at home. I feel butterflies and know I'm nervous. I choose a Dolly Parton tape because my mom has the record.

"Dolly Parton has the hugest boobs in the world," Melissa says looking over my shoulder.

"I know," I say. "I don't know how she walks with them."

Melissa goes first and we all scramble onto the couch for front row seats. Lisa presses play on the music box. Melissa holds the hairbrush up to her lips and pretends to actually sing the words through the whole song. At one point she pretends she's holding a note for a really long time and holds her head back as she sings.

Kelly says, "I'm next," after we stop clapping. She does the exact same dance as Melissa and lip-synchs to Irene Cara's "Fame." We all applaud when she finishes.

No one volunteers to go next and we sit in silence for a minute. I twirl my hair in my hand. I hope they're getting tired of the talent contest and move on to movies and eating pizza.

"Why don't you go, Molly?" Lisa says.

I look over at Nicole and she smiles at me from the other end of the couch. We sing in her room sometimes, so she says, "Get up there."

I jump up and hope an aggressive attack of the hairbrush microphone will make me feel less nervous. It doesn't. From my vantage point, I feel even more singled out. Everyone looks all cozy on the couch. Melissa and Nicole are practically hugging, they're so attached at the hip, and Kelly and Lisa moon over Nicole's pink sweater. At least they aren't staring at me yet, I think.

I ask Melissa to play Dolly Parton's song "Jolene." When she hits play, I close my eyes and totally lose myself in the music. Words that I don't think I know fly from my mouth. I catch myself actually singing the song – breaking the first rule of lip-syncing. I sway my arms and hips to the beat and, at the end of the song, I take a bow just like I've seen actors do in black and white musical movies. I actually feel really good even though I did really sing the song and not lip synch it.

"This is boring," Melissa says, and presses stop on the boom box. "Let's do something different."

I glare at her as I sit down and hug my knees into my body. The singing was actually a ton of fun. All that worry for nothing. Lisa whispers in Melissa's ear. Nicole gets a Coke from the mini-fridge and Kelly says, "We can make drawings."

"Nah," everyone says at once.

"I know," Melissa says. "Let's play truth or dare. But only after I open my presents."

Melissa's mom comes down as we put our gifts onto the coffee table. She sets a huge take-out pizza down next to the TV console.

"Thanks, Mrs. Meyer," we say in unison.

"I don't like pepperoni," Nicole says after Mrs. Meyer leaves the room.

"You do, too," I say. "We have pepperoni at your house all the time."

"Well, I don't like it anymore," Nicole says and gives me a look.

"Me neither," Lisa says. "I'm on a diet."

I laugh out loud because Lisa is the skinniest girl I've ever met. I grab a slice and notice her curly brown hair and blue eyes. She's wearing what I now know are Calvin Klein jeans and a t-shirt with a unicorn and glitter on it. She has pierced ears. Kelly's wearing jeans with Jordache on the back pocket. I've never seen those before. She has on a red shirt with the horse on it. She smiles as she eats her slice. Nicole and Lisa pick all the pepperoni off their slices. And, I notice how pretty Nicole looks in pink. I realize it's been a while since we mooshed each other.

All of a sudden, I feel ugly in my hand-me down Levi's and blue sweatshirt with hearts on the front. Even though it's my favorite sweatshirt, it feels too old. When I look at the other girls, they seem fresh and new. I wish I could look as pretty as them.

When we finish our pizza, we sit on the floor in a circle around the pizza box while Melissa opens her presents. The radio plays the local pop station in the background. Her gifts are all variations on the same present: nail polish, eye shadows, stickers of unicorns plus a horse figurine from Kelly. I grab another slice and glance at Nicole while I eat it pepperoni and all.

"Thanks guys," Melissa says. I notice that she set aside the blue nail polish I got her. I wonder if she likes it.

We sit in a circle and play a few rounds of Truth or Dare. It's pretty fun at first. Nicole has to eat dirt from a plant. Lisa gargles with water from the fish tank. Melissa runs upstairs to drink pickle juice with Nicole as her witness. Kelly tells us she sucked her thumb until third grade. I pick truth because I'm afraid of dares. So, when Melissa asks me if I've ever touched myself, I can't believe it. I feel my face get red and I look over at Nicole. She leans back on her hands and looks me right in the eyes.

"Eww. No," I answer and hope that will be the end.

"Come on, Molly." Melissa says. "I know you have."

I give her a look with slanted eyes. "What are you talking about?"

"You know." Nicole says. "Come on, we all do it. Just admit it."

I want to tell the truth, because I still believe there's nothing wrong with doing it. But I already lied, so I have to keep my answer. Plus, I remember that Nicole was grossed out when I told her about it and there's no way she ever did it. She wouldn't. But I guess she did tell Melissa I did.

"I said no." I clench my fists under my legs. I want to yell at Nicole, but I don't want them to think I lied.

"Well, I think you're lying," Melissa says. "Maybe you should do a dare too."

"I'm not lying, and I won't do a dare. Nobody else had to do two in a row."

"Let's just watch movies, Melissa." Kelly says. "Just leave her alone."

Everyone scrambles onto the sectional and Melissa gives me a backwards look. I stick my tongue out at her.

For the first time I'm glad I don't get to sit next to Nicole, even though we always sit next to each other when we watch TV together. Besides, she and Melissa are still attached at the hip and Kelly sits on the other side of her. I sit on the end of the couch scrunched next to the arm. I feel alone again and get stuck in my head wondering about when it became so important where you sat on a sofa and why it mattered so much who you liked and what you wore and what you did. I never had to worry about that kind of stuff so much before. I don't like it. Plus, I've never had to worry about Nicole telling people things about me. I feel confused.

Luckily, it's super neat to see Yoda on the big screen at Melissa's house.

By the time the movie is over, it's like we are all friends again. Lisa grabs my hand, turns to me, "I'm sorry that happened earlier. Sometimes Melissa can be too pushy."

"It's okay," I say even though I still feel mad. I don't want to feel that way, though, so I lie.

We all dig into our overnight bags for our sleeping gear. Lisa leaves the room to change into her long flannel nightgown with ruffles on the collar and flowers plastered all over it. She brushes her hair while she sits cross-legged on the carpet. Melissa takes off her shirt in front of all of us to prove that she really does have boobs, then she puts on her dad's green pants. He's an ER doctor and Melissa says, "they are his scrubs."

I face the wall and hurry to put on my t-shirt. Nicole has a big t-shirt too. Hers is different though because it's from her dad's firehouse. Everyone thinks it's so great that her dad is a fireman and asks her tons of questions about it. They want to know if he ever tells scary stories or if he's ever seen a dead person. Of course, I know he comes home and cooks to get his mind off his job and rarely talks about what he does for a living, just like Nicole's mom who is a nurse. But Nicole tells them a gruesome story about a boy her dad helped rescue a few years ago. The kid's arms burned to a crisp after he tried to climb from his burning house via the power line out of his window. I remember that story. I was there when her dad told it, but I didn't want to hear it again.

There's a lot of talk and commotion before we lay in our bags. I expect to sleep next to Nicole since we've been having sleepovers since we were six. But she is in-between Melissa and Kelly. And, Lisa is next to Kelly. I don't want to sleep next to Melissa, even though it's her birthday, so I put my bag on the end next to Lisa. I want to fall down laughing and giggling like the others. They make their happiness look so easy, so effortless. But, when I try join in, they won't let me. They scoot in closer together in the middle and I keep getting left out.

I feel so far away from everyone again. I want to say something, but when I open my mouth, I just want to cry. I don't want anyone to see me cry. As the girls whisper secrets and snuggle into their perfect sleeping bags, I try to ignore the smell of dad's loaner bag. Rather than admit that I want to sleep in the middle of two girls too, admit that I'm sad and mad that Melissa shut down the singing after I sang good, and that she asked me about a secret that I only told to Nicole, I curl into my bag, snuggle with my pink pillow and let the tears – the tears that waited all evening to flow – come as quietly as I could control them.

Throughout the night, I hear the others giggle and whisper to each other. I want to laugh too, but no one offers to include me in the joke, and I don't know how to jump in and just laugh. I think maybe, maybe if I try to giggle, just let laughter out of my mouth it will flow. Laughing will feel good, I think, but a muffled sob is all I have.

I don't think anyone can hear me. I try to relax and think about Nancy Drew, a girl everyone likes. I go into my imagination again. I have the cherry red convertible and my long hair flies in the breeze behind me as I drive around investigating mysteries and impressing everyone with my smart ideas. But that makes me even sadder, because I don't feel very smart for not knowing what to do in this situation. Eventually, I fall asleep.

Late at night, I sense them over me. I hear Melissa say, "Touch her hair. Let's put lotion in it." And, as they squirt goo in my hair, I lie there and pretend to be asleep. I think I will never let them touch me. No. I build shields in my head. I make vows to myself. All the while, I let them hurt me.

Much later it's quiet, I get out of my bag and tiptoe up the stairs to the bathroom with the newspaper print wallpaper. I wash my hair in the sink with hand soap. I scrub out all the evil lotion and remove the evidence. When I go back downstairs, Nicole, awake too, smiles at me with this "That's awful. I'm so sorry" look on her face. I don't smile back. I climb into my sleeping bag and bury my wet head in my pillow.

In the morning, I pretend everything is normal. We say our goodbyes and thank yous after eating donuts around the breakfast nook. I call Mom early just to be sure she picks me up first. I lie to the girls and tell them I have shopping plans with her.

As I walk out the door, Melissa whispers to Nicole again. They giggle. I run to the car, not sure what to say to Mom about my first and totally horrible slumber party.

"How was it?"

"Fine."

Dear Diary,

I just had the worst night ever. Why would Melissa invite me to her slumber party just to be mean to me? Did she know before the party? Did she plan it? Because she was so mean, I spent my first slumber party ever crying in my Lucy pillow. It wasn't anything like the times I stay over at Nicole's and we play Battleship, UNO and Space Invaders and sing along to Teddy's records. Does everyone hate me now? I hope not. Sad Molly.

At school on Monday, Nicole was the big star because now everyone knew her dad was a firefighter because of the t-shirt she wore to Melissa's slumber party. All the boys thought it was so cool and all the girls thought it was so cool that the boys thought it was so cool. Ms. Byers asked Nicole if her dad would like to come to the class to tell us all about his job. Nicole said she'd ask.

I thought it was so lame because all they did at the firehouse was sit around and make food for each other and play video games and clean the fire truck. But mostly I was just totally jealous of her. She got so much attention just because of something her dad did, because he saved lives and saw dead, burnt bodies. It wasn't even for something *she* did.

I remembered a time in second grade when Renee Goldstein got popular because her baby brother died. Everyone treated her differently. Before she'd just been this girl in our class with glasses and braces, then her brother died and all of a sudden, she was super popular. It wasn't like I wanted anyone in my family to die so I could get popular, I didn't even know if I wanted to be popular, I just wanted Nicole's attention. I didn't know if I'd ever get it again.

10

One rain-slicked afternoon, I came home from school to find my grandpa sitting in the big black chair in our living room reading the newspaper.

"Where's Mom?"

"At the hospital."

"No way! When?"

"A few hours ago. You and Colin are going to stay over at my house for the night."

Before he could say anymore, I skipped towards my room and yelled back. "I'll go pack."

In my room, I packed my favorite items and my diary and as I looked around my room, it dawned on me that life might be different in a matter of hours, days. I didn't know how long it took to have a baby or prepare it to bring home. I had ideas that it needed to be wrapped in a soft blanket like a cinnamon roll and that someone would whack it on the butt for some mysterious reason – I'd seen that on TV. But I really couldn't imagine having a live baby in my house. I wondered what Colin thought. Being over a year younger than me, he was totally clueless about the whole baby thing. I don't think Mom had given him a book about how babies were made, but I didn't ask either.

At Papa's house, Colin and I enjoyed the standard treats that came with staying the night at his house. He lived just two blocks away from us and Mom and Dad used his babysitting services whenever they could. But since Mom was pregnant, they never went out at night anymore. To Colin and me, staying over there was always like a luxury vacation. Papa treated us to the best of the best.

He made us a home-cooked dinner. It wasn't fancy or anything – just canned tomato soup and grilled cheese sandwiches. The best part was we used our own special plates and silverware that only we got to use. They were the plates, bowls, spoons and forks that my mom and her brother used when they were growing up. The plates and bowls were decorated with fuzzy red bears – like Goldilocks friends and just right. And the silverware was engraved on the handles with the alphabet. Slurping hot tomato soup was never as fun at home.

After dinner, we did our homework while Papa washed the dishes and prepared all the fixings for our ice cream sundaes. Visions of staying up late and eating ice cream sundaes with vanilla ice cream, maraschino cherries, chocolate fudge and crushed peanuts filled my sugar-deprived head.

I tried reading about copperheads of Indiana. I tried to be interested in their methods of attack and techniques for blending into their environments for both protection from their enemies and as a way of duping their prey. I wanted to be intrigued by their mechanisms of defense. But I couldn't help wondering about this baby.

"Hey Colin." I peered at him from across the dining table. "Do you think we'll have a brother or sister?"

"I dunno. I hope it's a boy and they call him Steve Majors."

"Why?"

"Because he's the Six Million Dollar Man. It'd be great to have a bionic brother."

I thought that if this kid, boy or girl, were a superhero like the ones we watched on TV on Saturday mornings while Mom and Dad slept, that maybe when it got older it could stop my parents from fighting. Maybe it would turn into the shape of an eagle and fly away and take us with it to live in its nest perched high in a tree surrounded by wooded mountains. Maybe it had a magic lasso like Wonder Woman. It could swing the lasso high above its head and gather Melissa in its rope so they couldn't escape. Maybe we'd all learn valuable lessons at the end of a half hour.

But most likely the baby would be regular just like Colin and me.

Reality looked more like I'd actually have to write and present a ten-minute talk on poisonous snakes instead of butterflies.

We got to watch TV while we ate our sundaes. I wanted to watch *Mork & Mindy* and for once I got my way! But Colin got to sit in Papa's cozy brown reclining chair, and I sat on the bright yellow davenport. I loved that he called his sofa a davenport and we called ours a couch. That word alone, davenport, made his house seem so far away to me. Like an escape.

After our sundaes, we put on our pajamas and brushed our teeth. He had a special stool in front of the sink just for us to stand on so we could reach the faucet ourselves. It had two steps and was wooden with carved alphabet blocks on the side – made just for kids. Even though I was tall enough to reach the sink on my own, I still used it because I'd been using it since I could remember.

Papa read us a story, one of us on either side of him on the davenport. I wish I could remember the story he read us that night – it was the night before everything changed and we became an even bigger family and I had to grow up in ways I would never have been able to predict. But I don't recall.

Papa was a big fan of prayers, so he encouraged Colin and I to recite, "Now I lay me down to sleep. If I should die before I wake, I pray the Lord my soul to take. Amen."

That prayer always gave me creepy feelings each time I said it. Why would I let anyone take my soul? But it was what we always said at Papa's house, so I always said it. At the end this time, though, I added silently to myself "And I hope it's a girl."

Papa turned off the lights and left the door open a crack. I thought about a sweet and soft baby girl to keep the scary soul-stealing thoughts out of my head.

The next morning Dad was there. He sat all casual on the piano bench with a cup of coffee between his hands while Papa lounged in his Lazy Boy recliner. His eyes shined happy and bright, but he looked heavy and tired … he wore a wrinkled blue button-down shirt that hung out of his pants like it was the shirt he wore the day before.

"Are you ready to be a big sister?"

"Yes," I ran up into his arms. "Yes.

He smelled funny – like he hadn't showered and had a film of dirt all around him.

"Well, you've got a little sister."

Colin came in rubbing his eyes with his fists.

"What's her name?" I felt like I might cry.

"Emma Drew. All her fingers and all her toes," Dad said in his latent Texan drawl.

We got to stay home from school, and I was relieved for the break. I realized I was tired from dealing with the girls at school and it was such a treat to visit Mom and baby Emma in the hospital. When I went up to the glass to look into the baby ward that was lined with metal and glass bassinettes, I clutched my stomach and shook a bit, afraid I would cry. A nurse held a baby bundled in white blankets with blue stripes. She brought the baby to the window and I saw that the baby was all bunched up and looked squished in her face. My heart raced and I jumped up and down as Papa watched me.

"I want to hold her. When can I hold her?"

"When she comes home from the hospital," he said.

My heart beat really fast and I was so excited, but I had to wait.

Mom and the baby stayed an extra day for observation. We stayed at home with Dad. We were totally out of food in the house and we were really hungry for dinner. Dad was clueless; we had to tell him to go to the grocery store.

At the grocery, Dad pushed the cart as me and Colin jumped all over each other. I kicked him hard in the shins after he punched me in the arm. Dad didn't scold us. And, I didn't feel bad.

"What do you kids eat anyways?"

"That," I pointed to the Fruity Pebbles cereal box.

"Yeah," Colin said. "Mom lets us have that for special times."

At home we gorged ourselves on super sweet cereal, ate in front of the TV, and stayed up way past our bedtime. I got a stomach ache and almost threw up but didn't – it was just like when it almost happens, and you accidentally swallow it so your throat hurts. I hate that. Colin and I thought we'd gotten away with a good one because Mom was always making us eat granola and Special K with soymilk. With Dad, we could do whatever.

I really wanted to call Nicole and tell her about the baby, but it was nice being at home when no one was fighting. And, we hadn't really been getting along really well since the slumber party, even though I still thought she was my best friend mostly because I didn't have anyone else to be close with.

Colin and I sat on either side of Dad's belly, leaning into him as we ate chocolate chip ice cream and watched *The Dukes of Hazard*. I wiggled my toes and watched my white socks fall off my feet and dangle at the tips.

I took my dish to the sink and sang, "clown feet clown feet. I have clown feet" as I skipped back. They didn't notice. Colin and Dad were like zombies in front of the television. They didn't say a word. I didn't think I was super funny or anything, but I just wanted them to see me and talk to me.

I gave them both a cold stare and stuck my tongue out at them. And, they still didn't notice. It sure will be nice to have another girl in the house, I thought. It was then that I realized – and it hit me like a ton of bricks – that I had a sister and I couldn't wait to have her home.

I went to bed early and read *Caddy Woodlawn*. It was next for our reading group and couldn't be worse than reading about snakes and their peculiar shedding habits. I shuddered at the thought of snakes. *Caddy Woodlawn*, so far, was about a girl my age growing up in pioneer times in Wisconsin. I liked that she was brave and talked to the Indians when everyone else seemed afraid of them. They're just people too, right?

I pulled the covers over me and twirled my hair with my fingers. Just as Caddy was off on her horse, a knock on my door startled me. It was Dad.

"You doing okay? You're quiet tonight."

Quiet, I thought. What about my clown feet? "I'm fine. I just want to be alone."

I looked him in the eyes, and he bent down to give me a hug. He smelled of Budweiser and un-brushed teeth.

"Your Mom will be home tomorrow."

"Goodnight."

"Goodnight baby girl."

The next day, Papa came over to watch us watch cartoons while Dad picked Mom and the baby up at the hospital. I sat on the carpet with my back to the couch and picked at the long brown shag carpet strands as Tom and Jerry fought over a waffle. Colin giggled and Papa read the paper.

I still wanted to call Nicole and tell her about the baby. So, I did.

My fingers shook as I dialed the number. That hadn't happened before; I tried to stop it with my other hand.

Nicole answered on the second ring. I didn't wait to say hello.

"She had a girl. Her name is Emma Drew."

"What's she like?" Nicole was excited and I felt comfortable and happy to talk to her like everything was normal again.

"I got to go to the hospital to see her yesterday. She's really little and cute. Blue eyes. But I didn't see her for long."

I paced around my parent's room as we talked on the phone.

"What'd I miss at school?"

"Melissa and Lisa got into a fight because Lisa talked to Kelly the night before, but she didn't call Melissa."

"That's stupid."

"Yeah, but you know Melissa. And Lisa left gym class crying."

"No way." I wondered who called Nicole besides me. No one else called me except Nicole.

"She was really upset."

"So, you wanna come over and see the baby later? Mom should be home soon."

"Ok. But maybe tomorrow. I'm going shopping with my mom now."

"Okay see you later."

I looked closely in the mirror to gaze at my green eyes and the freckles on my nose. I looked at my outfit. Old Levi's from cousin Shannon and a blue and white striped collared shirt that I only wished was alligator like the kids at school wore. I bit my nails. How come Nicole always got to shop with her mom? I never got new things. Her mom was so fun – they went on vacation and shopped, and Nicole never seemed to wear the same outfit twice. They lived on the same side of town as us. How come she had so much more?

I went to the kitchen and grabbed a bowl from the cupboard. I filled it to the rim with Fruity Pebbles before covering them with 2% milk and carried the bowl, slowly balancing it in my hands, to the couch. Papa looked up at me from his newspaper.

"Didn't you just have breakfast not an hour ago?"

"Yeah. I'm still hungry."

"Okay." He turned back to his reading as I sat on the floor next to Colin. The Super Friends had replaced Tom and Jerry.

A car honked outside, and we knew it was Mom and the baby. I watched Dad help Mom out of the big green station wagon. She had the baby in her arms, which made it difficult for her to get out of her seat. Slowly she made her way up the stone steps leading to the house. Dad carried her bags behind her.

Papa opened the door and Mom looked tired. Her eyes were droopy. But she had this glow around her as she stepped into the house.

"Candice. Can I take your sweater?"

"No thanks Dad. I'm all right."

Mom held the baby's neck as she laid her on the couch on her back. She was all bundled up in the blankets.

I sat on the couch next to the baby and looked at her while Mom took off her sweater.

"Can I touch her?"

"Sure. You can even hold her."

I put my hand on her hair. It was the softest thing I'd ever felt in my whole life. Softer than a strawberry leaf or probably a butterfly wing.

"Really?"

"Yes. Here." She adjusted the pillows on the couch so that one was under my left forearm and elbow. "Hold her so you can cradle her neck on the crook of your arm. You want to make sure you help her hold her head because she doesn't have strong muscles in her neck yet."

I felt the weight of her in my arms. She made gurgling noises as I touched her forehead very lightly with my fingers.

"She's so soft."

Mom smiled her tired smile at me while I held her, and I felt like I could sit there all day just staring at Emma's face.

"Can I unwrap her blanket and see her hands and fingers?"

"Sure."

Her skin felt even softer like the new terry cloth towels Mom bought for drying the baby – and those were the softest things I'd ever felt before I touched Emma's hair.

"I love her," I said and secretly to her and myself I said "I'll take good care of you. I promise."

Then it was everyone else's turn to hold baby Emma. Papa seemed to be an old pro. He knew all about watching her neck and holding her close. Colin looked the most awkward and he couldn't get his pillows adjusted right. He got frustrated and left the room saying he had to pee. Dad surprised me the most. He really looked comfortable holding her gently over his shoulder, burping her after Mom fed her with a bottle.

Maybe Dad was that sweet with me, I thought. Maybe he held me like that before I got too old to hold.

Dear Diary,

I have a little sister! Her name is Emma Drew Greely and I've never seen a prettier, sweeter baby. I love her!!! I hope Nicole loves her too. Maybe she won't be mad at me anymore — even though I didn't really know why she's mad anyways. Oh well. I love Emma and right now that's all that matters. But I do hope Monday at school is okay.

Love Molly.

The best big sister ever!

11

Now that Emma was around everything felt different around the house. We were no longer a family of just two kids and a mom and dad. Now there were five of us. And, after Papa went home, the idea of a new family sunk in more. The atmosphere at home wasn't like a special occasion anymore, like I felt when we had company over for Christmas. It felt real, like everyday life but with a new person. Like she was found on the doorstep or an alien ship dropped her off. We didn't know how to behave around her.

I couldn't help myself from just staring at her or touching her. Each time I walked into a room where her baby seat was set up, it felt strange to see her and I'd take a second look and notice her newness again. She even smelled brand new.

She was Mom's sidekick and always near her. She garbled strange noises and she cried a lot. I heard her at night. And even though she slept in a bassinette in Mom and Dad's room all the way down the hall, she'd wake me up in the middle of the night with her crying. Sometimes it took hours for her to sleep. I'd toss and turn in bed and wonder if I'd ever fall asleep. I didn't like her so much then, but I loved her and that was only the first few days.

And, one day she took over.

"You know, sweetie," Mom looked at me over spaghetti dinner while Emma slept in her baby chair on the floor next to the table. "With Emma crying so much in the night, I want her to have her own room closer to ours. We want to move Colin into your room and move her crib into his room. We'll set up the bunk bed in your room for you two. Won't that be fun?"

"What? You are kidding? I don't want to share my room."

Colin groaned and put his head in his hands.

"Well, I'm sorry. We have no choice," Mom said.

Colin stared at the wall over his plate. I left the table and ran to my room then slammed the door behind me. *This sucks*, I thought, *now I have to share a room with my stupid brother.*

Dear Diary,

The worst thing ever happened – I have to share a room with Colin. I'm so sad. Where will Nicole sleep when she spends the night? How will I change clothes in the morning? I've been good. I double pinky swear. So, why do bad things keep happening to me?

Sadder than ever, Molly

The next day Dad helped Colin move his Tonka trucks into my room. I sulked in the living room and read *Caddie Woodlawn*. I felt a little better since Caddie had a tough pioneer life but still kept her positive attitude. She acted brave about everything – even plowing a field or crossing an icy river on a horse. Things could be worse, I thought.

Mom napped while the baby slept, and I heard Dad yell "Goddammit" from my bedroom.

I set down my book and went to investigate. They had the bunk bed half assembled – just the bottom part. My whole room was a mess. I wanted to scream at them to clean it up, but when I noticed the sweat on Dad's forehead, I stopped myself.

Dad attached some screws while Colin stood over him. "Grab me that wide screwdriver."

"This one?"

"No. Hell." Dad scrambled up to his feet to dig in the toolbox. I looked to Colin. He stood next to the toolbox and backed up when Dad approached. Dad picked up the Budweiser can next to the toolbox and took a long sip. The phone rang and I was glad to leave them to answer it.

It was Nicole.

I said "hi" with a touch of surprise. She caught on and was super normal with me.

"Can I come over to see the baby now?"

"She's sleeping. Wanna go for a bike ride then come over after?"

"It's freezing outside."

"How about roller skating?" I had to get out of the house.

"Okay. I'll meet you halfway."

Ever since third grade when we got permission to leave our houses without one of our parents around Nicole and me always met halfway. We each walked 335 baby steps to meet exactly equal distance from each other's house. That way no one ever had to walk, or skate, or ride a bike further than the other. As we grew the number of steps decreased with the increase of our shoe size, so we always met in the middle of the block of 64th and Garland in front of the brown house with the black shutters and the big maple tree in the front yard.

I shuttered in the crisp air and I was so glad I wore a jacket over my cable knit sweater. I felt my face red with heat and sweat from roller-skating over. I loved my skates. They were blue sneakers attached to wheels – with laces and everything. They were my most prized possession. On warmer days, I wore my special roller-skating jacket. It was light blue sateen with a silvery glitter roller skate on the back. I felt like a roller-skating queen in my jacket and aside from softball, which I had played since I was seven, roller-skating was my best sport.

When I saw Nicole at our special meeting place it felt like a whole other world where babies didn't exist. A world that hadn't changed.

She smiled and seemed really happy to see me. She grabbed my hand. "So, what's she like?"

"Small."

"Does she cry a lot?"

"Sometimes."

"When can I see her?"

"Later. Let's skate." I said as I let go of her hand and skated in the direction of our favorite smooth spot in the street. Even though I felt like I could trust her again and everything felt normal, I didn't want her to get to have everything her way. But I didn't want to be mean about it – just normal. I looked over my shoulder and chatted with Nicole along the way. "It's so weird having a baby in the house. Ugh, I got terrible news today."

"What? Tell me," Nicole caught up to me and put her arm in mine. We skated together.

"I have to share a room with Colin."

We slowed down to go over a bump in the pavement.

"That is horrible," she said. "I'd hate to share a room with Teddy."

"He'd hate it more," I teased, and we laughed.

We preferred a side street that was recently paved. It was effortless to skate there – no potholes or bumpy repairs to the road. I skated backwards and pretended I was in a figure-skating championship – except my vision of how I wanted to move and do a leap and twist didn't match what I did. I almost tripped and caught myself before I fell.

"Gosh. It just totally sucks."

"I know. It's gross. He has boy things like trucks and robot posters"

"They won't match your butterflies," Nicole said.

"I know. My room is going to get all uglied up. Why are boys so weird?'

Nicole and I grabbed hands and spun each other in a circle – going around and round. When we let go, we did a matching pirouette and finished the move with an Olympic ice-skating finish – one foot back behind the other in a curtsey.

Nicole caught her breath. "Not all boys are weird. I can think of a few that aren't so bad."

"Yeah? Like who?"

"Mike Spangler is one. He's just so cute." Nicole clasped her hands in front of her almost like she was praying.

"He's okay," I said watching Nicole smiles as she thought of him.

He was the absolute best-looking boy in our class. I thought of Mike as an untouchable. He was blond with blue eyes, and he didn't talk loud at lunch like Mark and Kevin. He was soft. I didn't see him acting like Kevin and Mark, so it was hard to think about him and Nicole going with each other or him going with anybody. He was just a boy. But I guessed we were supposed to like boys to go with. I just didn't want Nicole to go with Mike. I didn't know why. I just didn't.

In the few short months we'd been at our new school, Nicole had become one of the most popular girls in the class without any effort. I didn't know how she did it, but I think it has something to do with the fact that she laughed at just about everything. And as much as I loved her, because I always had, I was so mad that it wasn't me who got instant popularity and felt a tinge of jealousy in my words.

"Well, I like him." Nicole blushed and did another turn on her skates.

I grabbed her hand and said, "I'm cold. Let's go back to my house and see if the baby is awake."

We left our skates on the front porch and walked into a house full of noise. The baby cried. Dad yelled from a distant room "Candice, where are my pliers?" The TV blared the news in the living room, but no one was watching. We found Mom in her room feeding the baby.

"Come sit down." She patted the bed next to her and Nicole and I climbed up to meet her. Mom smiled at Nicole who was staring at the feeding baby. "You can hold her when she's done."

"Really?"

"I'll show you how," Mom said.

Nicole and I cooed at the baby and watched Mom change her diaper. Emma had this brown, worm-like, gooey thing on her belly button.

"Eww, gross. What's that?" I asked, afraid to touch it.

"That's what'd left of her umbilical cord. It was how I fed her while she grew in my belly. Eventually it will scab then fall off."

"Like when my knee got a scab after I fell off my bike?" I asked.

"Exactly like that."

"Did I have an unbilical cord?" I asked.

"It's *umbilical*, and of course." Mom smiled and snapped the baby's clothes together before she bundled her up in the blankets. I lifted my shirt to look at my belly button and Nicole did the same. We giggled.

"So, is this umbilical cord the same as the belly button?" I said.

"A little bit. When the scab falls off and the skin heals, the belly button is what's left."

Mom looked at Nicole and me as she handed Emma off to Nicole and showed her how to hold her arms together to protect Emma's neck. As I watched her nervous attempts to hold the baby right, I saw her not as the most popular girl in school and the girl who was sure to get to go with the cute boy in our class, but as my oldest friend. The girl I'd known for as long as I could remember.

"I have an innie," Nicole said.

"Me too! Colin has an outie. Why is his different?"

"I don't know sweetie. That's just the way his grew."

"What kind will Emma have?"

"We'll just have to wait and see."

Nicole and I left Mom to nap with the baby. We went to inspect my room. It was so different. The bunk bed was where my bed used to be, and my bed was gone. The bunk bed was huge and made my room seem so much smaller. Its dark wood didn't match the flowered wallpaper. Dad was in the baby's new room setting up the crib. Colin sat on the floor and organized his scattered matchbox cars and trucks. My Lucy pillow was on the lower bunk.

"I want the top bunk." I grabbed my pillow, climbed the ladder to the top and exchanged it for Colin's Star Wars pillow. "I'm the oldest, so I get to say."

"No way. This is *my* bed. I get the top."

"Mom! Colin won't let me have the top bunk." My voice filled the room. I clenched my fists at my sides and felt my face grow hot. My whole upper body was tense, and I felt like I wanted to hit Colin, just tackle him, but I stopped myself when Dad rushed in to shush us.

"Your mother and the baby need to rest so shut it." Dad bent over to collect his toolbox and empty beer can from the floor. He smelled sweaty like he needed to take a shower.

"Dad, Colin won't let me sleep on the top bunk, but I'm oldest and I think I should get to pick first."

"But it's my bed."

"It's my room."

"Dad!" He turned to us both and Nicole side stepped into the corner of the room to investigate Colin's comic book collection that lay spread on the floor.

"Shit, why can't you kids work it out? Who was here first?"

"I was," Colin said.

"Then it's yours."

"That's totally unfair," I said and crossed my arms over my chest. "He was in here all day."

"Life is unfair," Dad said as he left the room.

"I should probably go home." Nicole said. "My Grandma's making supper."

"Do you want me to skate halfway with you?"

"No thanks. I can do it myself." The air in the room stopped circulating.

"Okay. See ya tomorrow at school." I walked her to the front door.

"See ya. Wouldn't want to be ya."

We laughed and Nicole left. I felt like a total idiot. She probably wanted to go home because she was uncomfortable with the arguing. No one ever seemed to argue at her house. Even though she and Teddy pretended to fight every once in a while, it was never about anything serious. Maybe I broke the spell of our great day, I wondered. I was so mad at Dad and Colin for making me look like a sissy who couldn't even get what she wanted in her own room.

I sat down on my bottom bunk and hugged my Lucy pillow. *Yeah, no one wants to be me*, I thought as I looked at my new environment. *No one wants to share a bedroom with a dumb brother.* I pulled the comforter through the slats that held the top bunk in place and made a tent over my head. I rolled onto my side and closed my eyes. I just wanted to start the day over.

I woke groggy to the smell of grilled cheese outside my tent. The dim light of evening was all around me and I shivered as I dismantled my makeshift tent. Mom was in the kitchen making grilled cheese and tomato sandwiches. Dad and Colin sat on the couch with a big orange comforter over them. I heard sounds of a basketball game on the television – cheering fans and the squeak of shoes on the court.

"I know it's not much." Mom said and handed me a plate with a sandwich. "I'm really tired sweetie. Did you have a nice nap?"

"Yeah." I set the plate on the table, sat down and rubbed my eyes. "Where's the baby?"

"Oh, she's sleeping in her new room."

Mom rubbed my head and kissed my cheek. She called Colin and Dad to dinner and we sat as a family at the dining table. It was pitch black outside at only six o'clock and there was a heavy feeling in the room. Dad ate his sandwich in less than five seconds, fidgeted in his chair and got up to watch the game. Colin picked at his food and tore the crusts off the bread and moved the pieces around his plate. I wondered how everyone could be so quiet with huge newness all around us.

Colin and I ate in silence. Mom cleared the dishes. The minutes dragged on as if in slow motion.

"Did you finish your homework?" Mom asked.

"We don't have any. We weren't in school on Friday. Remember? And, it's only Saturday" I said.

"Oh right." She went to get the baby and returned with her over her shoulder. She rubbed her back and the baby cooed. I still couldn't believe I had a baby sister and she was a little girl and her name was Emma. I watched everyone in silence.

Mom moved about in a new way – with the baby attached to her – or with the baby that was no longer attached to her but waiting for her belly button to grow.

I thought about butterflies and snakes. Butterflies started as caterpillars, made cocoons and once they were old enough to be butterflies, they tore down or chewed their way out of the cocoon and flew away. Snakes shed their skin as they aged. They grew just as I was growing and changing and just like Emma's umbilical cord would change. And, just like Nicole changed at school.

12

Monday was my first day back to school post new sister and it felt more different than ever before. First, I had to listen to Nicole's mom ask all kinds of questions about Emma while we drove to school – like what I thought about her and did I like being a big sister. The whole ride to school was about the baby.

In Room 12, Ms. Byers usually sat at her desk and smiled as us kids walked into class. When I entered, she stood up, walked over to me and told me I didn't miss "anything vital." She said she was excited to hear about the new arrival and she hoped I'd found time to do some snake research over the weekend, despite all the excitement.

Everyone talked about their weekend as they put their things away in the coat closet. A few kids had gone away with their parents, some had stayed at the house of the parent they didn't live with, some saw movies – but no one else had a new family member come into their life. I was excited to have news to share.

"My mom had a baby over the weekend." I put my hat and coat on the rack and looked into the void. No one was there. They'd all left the coatroom to take their seats.

When we had to use our dictionary word of the day: *entrance – to fill with delight, to enchant*, in a sentence, I wrote, *I'm entranced with my new baby sister.*

I had imagined that I'd be greeted at the door of the school with flowers or at least a barrage of pats on the back – congratulations of some sort. It seemed word spread quickly at the school and that everyone should be aware by now that something completely extraordinary had happened over my weekend. But no one seemed to notice I was absent on Friday except Nicole and Ms. Byers.

When we got in line for gym class, I stood next to Melissa and told her my news.

"Really," she smiled wide and flipped her long black hair away from her face. "My mom is pregnant too and she's supposed to have her baby over the summer."

"Oh, that's cool." I wished I had hair to flip back like Melissa. Her hair was like magic. Her hair *entranced* the boys in our class, I thought. Then I thought of Nicole and her blond hair and Mike and his blond hair, which made me think about what color hair Emma will have. Mine was cut short and was supposed to look like a famous ice skater's hair, but it never really looked as good as hers.

Nicole was two people ahead of me in line and stood right behind Mike Spangler. She laughed with Lisa. I wondered what they laughed about, and I tried to catch her attention by making the pssst sound under my breath, thinking I'd try to make her laugh and get her attention. She caught my smile and looked away. She didn't even smile back. I wondered what was up her butt.

Once we got to the gym all the kids ran off in a billion different directions while Ms. Garth blew on her whistle.

I asked her if I could sit out. "I'm not feeling well." I added, then rubbed my belly.

"Well, Molly, what's wrong? I hear you just became a big sister."

"How did you know?"

"We got a call to tell us why you weren't in class."

"Oh. Yeah. I have a little sister now. She's really cute."

"So, what's wrong?"

"I'm just tired. I didn't sleep really good last night."

"Really *well*," she corrected me. "Well a little exercise should make you feel better, don't you think?"

"Yeah, but ..." She wouldn't let me finish and talked over my words.

"Very well, go take your place with the others. We'll start with a game of dodge ball, children." I was surprised such a high-pitched drawl could come from such a large woman.

The squeaky sound of shoes on the gym floor filled the room. Ms. Garth was prone to walking with a limp and she had a large chest we called the uni-boob behind her back. I wondered what size bra she wore. She grabbed two red balls from a locked cabinet and held them at her waist.

"Let's count off in ones and twos to divide into teams."

I didn't want to play. I didn't want to run around a room just to get hit with a ball. Plus, the boys always took the game so seriously.

I turned to Lisa. "What's up with her uni-boob today? It's got a life of its own."

"I know. Where does she buy her clothes?"

"She doesn't wear clothes. She wears a tent over her shoulders."

Ms. Garth blew the whistle and the game was on. I ran around the gym with my eye on one red ball in play knowing that soon there would be two. The rule was if you could catch the ball as it was thrown at you, the person who threw it was out; but if you didn't then you were out. I didn't care if I was in or out, I just didn't want to get hit.

Most of the class ran in circles around the perimeter of the gym to avoid harm. Mark had the ball and he threw it at Jane who everyone knew couldn't catch. Then Mike picked up the ball and tried to hit Kristi who was one of the best athletes in our class. She caught the ball and Mike was out.

Since I'd kept to the outside rim of my team's side, near the end of the game I was still a contender and had yet to touch the ball. Nicole picked it up and even though she was on the opposite team, I thought I was safe because I knew she'd never try to hit me. I stood close to the back of the red line as she bounced back and forth near the center, looking for a target. I slipped past her gaze and a moment later, I felt a sharp pain on my backside. I'd been hit – by Nicole.

After class, I made sure to stand next to her in line for the walk back to our classroom.

"What'd you hit me for?"

"It's just a game Molly."

"Well, it hurt."

She turned to Melissa and whispered in her ear. They looked back at me and laughed.

At lunch Kelly and Melissa sat on either side of Nicole and I sat next to Lisa at the end of the table. They laughed about some TV movie they'd all watched with their moms. I hadn't seen it. I tried to chime in with a reference to one of the books we'd read for class and they all turned to look at me.

"That book is for school," Melissa said. "Not for fun. Don't you ever watch movies?"

"Not last weekend," I said. I took a bite of my baloney sandwich. "I was busy."

"Her mom had a baby. So cute," Nicole said. She pinched Kelly's cheeks, and everyone laughed.

Lisa said, "I love babies." I turned to her and smiled. She smiled back and ate another Cheetos.

"I hope she grows up to be cuter than Molly," Melissa said.

Melissa and Kelly laughed, and Nicole shrugged her shoulders and smiled at me like she was making an apology.

I got mad at them all. I was so tired, and it was hard to think of something good to say back. I wanted to burn Melissa with my words. But the bell rang, and we all got up to go back to class.

The rest of afternoon I struggled to stay awake and wondered why Nicole hit me in gym class and why she acted so different at home than she did at school. Luckily when Ms. Byers called on me during our geography lesson, I knew the capitol of New York was Albany and I didn't vomit on her desk.

After school, I ran into the house and let the door slam behind me. The shades were up, the curtains open and Mom's book was open on the couch. But the house was still like no one was home.

"Mom," I yelled.

It was weird because Mom usually greeted me at the door by telling me about the after-school snack she had ready for us. Sometimes, she even sang along with Barbara Streisand as she put a plate of celery and peanut butter with raisins on the dining table. She called them ant logs. But on this day, there was nothing. I felt cold and alone.

Suddenly, I missed my room. I wanted to write in my diary about all the weirdness, but Colin was in there playing with his Matchbox cars. I left him alone and didn't even say hi. I wanted to find Mom. I wanted a hug.

Mom and the baby were asleep in Mom and Dad's room. I went to the bed and noticed how deeply Mom slept. Her breathing was faint, and she looked strange to me without her glasses on. Her blond hair was matted down on her head and she looked both older and younger. Emma lay next to her breathing more quickly. Her eyes fluttered as she lay on her back.

I bent over to kiss her lightly on the forehead. She jumped awake and I backed away startled.

"Oh sweetie. I didn't hear you come in. Are you hungry? I'll make you a snack." She put her glasses back on and smoothed her hair with her fingertips.

"That's okay. Go ahead and sleep some more. I can make my own snack."

"Ok." She closed her eyes and drifted right back to sleep. Her glasses still on her face.

A while later, Colin and I watched *Tom and Jerry* and I heard the baby wail from the bedroom. It freaked me out like the sound of a fire truck screeching down our quiet street. I guessed I was going to have to get used to it. I went into the bedroom and asked if I could help.

She'd stopped crying when I got there, and Mom jumped at the sound of my voice. "Oh, you scared me. Nope, thanks, all done." She put Emma on her shoulder and walked with me back to the living room. "One thing you can do is hold her while I get dinner started."

I held her in my arms as I'd been taught to do. It was becoming more and more natural to me which was confusing because in some ways I wanted Mom to be like she was when she was awake and made us cookies after school and in some ways, I thought it was pretty neat I was learning how to hold a baby and get to know this totally new person.

"How was school today?"

I thought about how Nicole hit me with the ball and what a jerk Melissa was, but I didn't want to tell Mom about it. "Fine," I said. I looked down at Emma's face. She had the smallest lips I'd ever seen.

"And what about you Colin? Come here and give me a hug."

"It was okay. Brian McKnight brought a real deer skull into show and tell."

"Gross," I said. "Where did he get it?"

"At Eagle Creek. They went hiking and found it."

"Was there blood?" I asked.

"No, idiot. It was bones."

I stuck my tongue out at him and he turned back to the tv.

Later at dinner, Colin and I ate hamburgers and peas alone while Mom fed Emma in the living room. The phone rang and I heard Mom talk low.

"That was your Dad. He has to work late tonight. The job hit some snags."

Colin and I finished our homework after dinner. Normally, we got to watch an hour of tv before our baths, but Mom was too busy with the baby to mention the bath and I didn't remember until the news came on.

"Are you still up? Where's your father?"

I shrugged my shoulders.

"Let's get you two to bed. Did you take your baths?"

"No," I said.

"Well, you're old enough now to do it yourself and I'd like you to start tomorrow, okay? You'll just have to go to school without a bath."

"I'd rather get up early for a bath, Mommy," I said.

"Okay, I'll wake you up early. Now scoot."

In bed I thought about Nicole and what I'd done wrong. I wondered if she was mad at me for something and that's why she hit me so hard. Maybe she did it because it was the strategic thing to do. But she could have tried to hit Lisa or even Adam. Maybe she wanted to get my attention. I thought maybe Melissa dared her to do it. It was just the kind of thing she would do. She could be so mean. Maybe her meanness rubbed off on Nicole.

Colin snored above me. I imagined I was deep in a cave hunting a leprechaun. I imagined I caught one and he showed me the way to his pot of gold at the bottom of the rainbow in a green meadow. I imagined I used the money to buy my parents a bigger house so I could have my own room.

The sound of tires on our gravel driveway woke me up. From my bedroom window, I watched Dad get out of his truck. He must've tripped on a rock because he practically fell into the front door. I heard it slam behind him and took a deep breath. I was glad he was home at last.

The next day, when Nicole and her mom picked me up for school, Nicole had a covered cardboard box on her lap.

"What's that?" I asked as I got into the car.

"Cupcakes." She said with a wide smile. Her blue eyes sparkled in the morning light.

"What for?" I asked.

"Just cause. Mom and I made them last night and we didn't want to keep them around the house. I thought I'd bring one for everyone in the class. I made this one special for you."

She decorated it with a jellybean flower. She didn't say a word about dodge ball. But I took the cupcake to mean she was sorry.

Dear Diary,

Nicole gave me a cupcake today. It had yellow, green and pink jellybeans on it, and it tasted so good. I ate it instead of my baloney sandwich at lunch. I'm sick of baloney sandwiches. I think we're friends again and I'm so happy everything is back to normal. Even Melissa was nice today. Are things getting better?? I hope so.

Love, Molly

13

A big storm hit right before Christmas vacation. Snow and rain created sleet and ice that closed businesses and schools. Me and Colin sat in front of the tv in the mornings and watched the news for the school closure announcements to come across the bottom of the screen, waiting for "All IPS Schools." It was rare to get out of school for a snowstorm, but sleet and ice were too dangerous, I guess. Day after day, they announced our schools were closed. We loved it.

The trees in our front yard looked bare covered in ice. A big wind downed some of the branches and others fell from their own icy weight. It looked like a twisted winter wonderland and Colin and I couldn't wait to play in the debris. We made forts and eagle nests and spent hours designing structures with icy twigs. I hit Colin on the cheek with an icy twig when he wouldn't get out of my nest. It kinda felt good to do it, so I pretended it was an accident. He didn't talk to me for the rest of the day, but I didn't care. I had my own fun.

Emma grew fast and after a month, she could hold up her own head. She cooed and laughed and seemed to have a real personality. She didn't scream as much as she did when she was a newborn. I tried to enjoy her.

Christmas was on the way. I used a crisp piece of Mom's flower stationery to make a list of stuff I wanted. I wrote with perfect printed words and threw away a few mistakes before I settled on my wish list. I felt that my needs were few and specific. I wanted: a monogrammed crewneck sweater, two Nancy Drew mysteries to fill in those missing from my collection, a Solid Gold record and a curling iron for when my hair grew out.

I gave my note to Mom. She was on the couch reading, her eyes partially open, half asleep.

"I made my Christmas list."

"You know Santa will do the best he can." She mumbled.

"I know. But I really want a monogrammed sweater, okay?"

She smiled just slightly. "We'll see."

"And a curling iron."

"But you don't even have long hair." She opened her eyes.

"I'm growing it out."

"I love it short." She sat up.

"I just want something different," I said.

Mom sighed, "Santa will do the best he can." She went back to reading her book. I went to call Nicole to see if she wanted to play in the icy trees with us.

Nicole answered the phone. "I can't. We're going Christmas shopping. I wanted you to come over here. But I guess I have to go shopping."

I felt sad. I wanted to get out of the house and away from the baby, Mom, Colin, our room – but I didn't have anywhere to go and no way of getting anywhere if I did. So, I went to my room to read, but ended up just taking a nap.

The days before Christmas were a blur of ice and stick sculptures. When Colin and I couldn't go outside, we played with Emma and showed her things in the house. I didn't feel like hitting him when we played with Emma. But, sometimes, when we played alone in our bedroom, I punch him if he cheated at Monopoly or UNO where before I'd just cheat too. Sometimes, I used my interviewing skills to teach Emma about the plants, the rooms and the appliances. She loved the mirrors. I loved introducing her to her. We watched the snow fall and drank hot chocolate. We made Shrinky Dink ornaments for the tree.

Dad drove us all to a big lot to get a tree. He made a scene over the price and Mom waited with Emma in the car. When we got home, Dad set it up on top of the coffee table that Mom had moved under the bay window.

I told Emma about all our special ornaments – a sparse assortment of homemade decorations Colin and I made over the years and a handful of store-bought ones. Dad put the angel on top of the tree. It was made of cardboard and covered in a silky fabric. At night, the tree glimmered with red, green, yellow, orange and white lights.

Papa always stayed at our house on Christmas Eve. It was a tradition for as long as I could remember. We drank eggnog and got to open one present each.

Colin and I snuggled with Papa on the couch. Dad sat in the big black chair and Mom sat on the brown shag carpet with Emma on her lap. I sipped my warm eggnog and felt the warmth of the mug expand into my palms and fingertips.

Dad handed the first present to Colin. He ripped through the Santa clad paper to reveal, surprise, another Tonka truck. My bedroom already looked like a junkyard and I was not pleased to see this addition. He rolled it across the floor and admired it most of the night.

Mom opened a present from me. It was a potholder that I bought at the school Santa Sale. It had a daisy embroidered on the hand. She smiled and gave me a quick hug with Emma still in her arms.

When my turn came, Mom gave me a small box. I shook it. It didn't make any noise. I pulled away the tape from each side very carefully and I opened the small wooden box. Inside was a gold ring in the shape of a heart with the initials MAG engraved in the front center. I put it on my right ring finger and held out my hand to admire it. It fit perfectly. It wasn't on my list, but I was so happy to have a surprise. I still wanted a monogrammed sweater. But I felt special, like surprises could happen to me.

"Thanks. It's so pretty. I love it."

"Your Papa picked it out," Dad said. He smiled at me from across the room.

I gave Papa a long hug and squeezed his arm before I let go.

"Thank you. I love you," I said.

"I love you too." He smiled and winked at me.

Christmas morning, I woke up before anyone else and went straight to the living room. The coffee table overflowed with the remaining presents and a few spilled onto the floor. My stocking bulged on the mantel and I took it down to investigate. It was filled with pencils, socks, a movie pass, a pack of gum and a rainbow bookmark.

Mom came in the room and saw me cross-legged on the carpet, chewing gum, and scolded me.

"I wish you would have waited to open your stocking till everyone was awake."

"But the stocking is nothing."

She gave me a look that said, "What did you just say?" Her eyes popped out of her head as she stood still with her hands on her hips.

"I'm sorry. It's just, I couldn't wait."

Once everyone was awake, we ripped through our presents. The room was a mess of discarded wrapping paper and bows. I got a sweater that I wished was red but was green. I got two Nancy Drew books. But I didn't get a curling iron or the Solid Gold album. I sat in the black chair and skimmed my new books trying to ignore Mom as she collected all the decent bows to use next year and Dad put the paper into the fireplace to help build the fire. I didn't say a word about the missing gifts and held my anger inside. I'll just not talk to her all day, I thought to myself.

When the phone rang, I knew it was Nicole. We always talked at Christmas after we'd both opened our presents. I jumped up to answer it.

"Merry Christmas s," she said. Her voice all sing-songy.

"Merry Christmas." My voice was not sing-songy. But I tried to sound happy.

"How many presents did you get," she asked.

"Five big ones and some little stuff."

"I got fifteen presents! Teddy and I had so many, that they filled up the whole living room."

"Wow. What did you get?" I asked as I bit my nails. I was so jealous.

"I got Life the Game, four sweaters, new roller skates, a stuffed butterfly that is so cute, beads to make a necklace, some records, a new tennis racket, skis, and some other stuff. What about you?"

"I got a sweater that my mom's gonna get monogrammed for me, a couple Nancy Drew books and a ring from my Grandpa. And some other stuff." I added that last part to make it seem like a lot.

"Neat. Ask if you can come over to play tomorrow because we're going to Colorado to go skiing the next day. We'll be gone for a week!"

"Okay." As I hung up the phone, I thought about how fun it'd be to go skiing. Or just go on a vacation at all. I didn't know how to ski. I'd never tried, and we'd only ever been on one vacation and that had been a weekend in Chicago to visit Mom's aunt a few summers ago. I remembered a musty apartment full of old, worn chairs and that the firemen came to the street to open the hydrant to let kids play in the water because it was so hot. Mom and Dad went to the King Tut exhibit and Colin and I sat at her aunt's house. It was a pretty boring vacation. I bet skiing was way more fun.

"Is Nicole having a nice Christmas," Mom asked.

"Yeah. Her presents filled the whole den. And they're going to Colorado to ski. Can I go to her house tomorrow to play?" So much for not talking to her all day, I thought. I couldn't even do that right.

"Well, it sure sounds like they're having fun over there. Yeah. I'll ask your Dad to take you over tomorrow."

Emma cried and Mom picked her up off the blanket she'd set up for her on the carpet. I sat on Papa's lap so he could hug me.

Dad drove me the few blocks to Nicole's house the next day. He didn't talk – only whistled. The radio was off, and he made his own tune. I stared out the window. When we got to Nicole's, I blew him a kiss and jumped out of the truck.

I rang the doorbell and Nicole and Barney greeted me at the door. Nicole grabbed my hand and pulled me through the living room and kitchen into the den. I caught a glimpse of the Christmas tree with a few stray presents underneath and four sets of skis that leaned against the wall in the living room. Four suitcases sat next to them. I wanted to go on a winter vacation.

Teddy was in the den, on the floor, playing with his new Collecovision. We watched him play Space Invaders. Everything felt normal over there, but part of me couldn't figure out if I was trying to act over normal and pretend it was normal when it really wasn't. I was confused. I felt different, but nothing at her house felt different.

We played teams against Teddy and I even managed to get the high score. I was feeling pretty good. The phone rang and Nicole jumped up to grab it. She went into the pantry behind the kitchen to talk. Usually she talked in the den in front of everyone. When she returned, I asked who it was.

She hesitated and smiled, so I knew she would lie to me. She always smiled when she lied. "No one."

"Come on. You were in there forever." I cajoled her.

"Really. It was a wrong number."

I let it go. I didn't want to fight over Christmas. Plus, I didn't know why she'd lie to me. So, I just let it go.

We went to her room to listen to the records she got. She showed me her new ski jacket and a curling iron. I suggested we curl each other's hair. Mine was really short, but I wanted to try anyways.

The phone rang again while we curled my hair. This time Teddy yelled from the den that it was for Nicole. She left and I continued curling my bangs. The curling iron was too big to curl them right, I needed a pencil thin iron for that. So, my bangs looked too crooked and some pieces didn't curl all the way and stuck up all weird.

By the time Nicole got back, I looked like her grandma just awake from a nap. Super small curls looked terrible on me, I decided. It was probably best that I didn't get a curling iron. I ran my fingers through my hair hoping to smooth them out.

"Who was that?" I asked.

"Melissa." She said as she turned over the record.

"What's she doing?"

I wondered why no one ever called me. Melissa didn't. I wouldn't have anything to say to her if she did, but I was jealous she called Nicole. I wasn't used to her getting so many phone calls while I was over at her house. I was used to having her all to myself.

"Nothing much." She opened her closet to fetch the Game of Life so we could set it up to play.

"Why'd she call?" I picked the red car.

"She just wanted to ask me something." She chose the blue one.

"Yeah. What?" I spun a six.

"Just something about Mike Spangler." Nicole spun a three.

I got to go first.

"What about him?" I was going to be a lawyer.

Nicole blushed. She spun and became a doctor. "He wants to go with me. Melissa called to ask me if I wanted to go with him."

I felt my heart skip a beat. I was both excited for and envious of her.

"I told her yes." She giggled. I wondered why Melissa was involved in this whole thing, but I saw the pattern. When a boy wants to go with you, he has a girl ask you for him. That's what Lisa did with Will and me, only Will didn't really want to go with me. I hated that I remembered that.

I spun and landed on four kids and put them in the car.

14

When school started after the New Year, the streets and yards lost their charm and winter wonderlandness. Former blinding white snowdrifts became slush piles black from exhaust. Trails of footprints and the icy remains of snow angels littered our yards. A dreary sheen covered the city as the days grew colder and colder. To me, January is like a sunken feeling. It's like you're in a hole deep in the ground and you have to make your way through dark shadows to emerge from a dirt cocoon.

Kids at school wore warm woolen crewnecks and corduroy pants tucked tightly into waterproof boots. Mom gave me a plastic bag so I could store my slush-appropriate boots after I changed into my indoor, school loafers. My new monogrammed sweater was perfect, and I wore it as often as I could. I loved to run my fingers over the raised initials while I stared out the windows. My monogrammed sweater was the one thing I had that made me feel like I fit in – rather than being a fashion misfit with hand-me-downs.

One day, as we were walking down the hall towards the music room, I overheard Melissa and Kelly talking.

"I know. She wears it every day," Melissa said.

"Yeah. She doesn't have to broadcast how poor she is," Melissa said. She passed Kelly a note and gave me a backwards look. Then she flipped her feathered hair.

I hated when she did that. Were they talking about me?

In music class, I sat next to Nicole and watched her play her cello. I had problems correlating and connecting how the notes on the page translated to the notes on the strings of my cello, so I liked to watch Nicole's fingers move and press the strings as we learned "Mississippi River."

"Are you copying me?" Nicole asked. She tried to scoot her seat just slightly away from mine, but she had trouble because our cellos were attached to our chairs via the board that kept our cellos from sliding across the floor as we held them upright.

"No. I'm just watching how you do it." I pushed the bow across the strings.

"Why are you so into what I'm doing? You just want to be like me. It's so annoying."

"No, I don't. I just want to play the cello." I said in a loud whisper.

"Shh. Girls. Be quiet over there." The teacher said over the sound of the class struggling to play in unison. The room sounded like a wild band of elephants in a fight.

I was so mad at Nicole and Melissa and even Kelly and so sick of the way they acted. I wanted to hit Nicole in the arm, but I didn't want to get in trouble at school. I kept quiet instead, but I made a promise to myself to get back at her somehow and prove I was not copying her.

That night we had to take our instruments home for practice. This was usually tricky because Nicole and I both played the cello and we had to fit them both into one of our parents' cars. On this particular day, Nicole's mom picked us up from school and she drove a Volkswagen Beetle, probably one of the world's smallest cars, which made the whole process doubly difficult. Plus, Barney was in the front seat when her mom arrived. He drooled dog slobber all over so Nicole and I both had to sit in the backseat with our cellos.

As we maneuvered our cellos into the car, I felt that familiar rush of anger sweep over me. My arms tightened. I felt a meanness fill my blood. After an afternoon of thinking about how mad I was at her, I felt like I wanted to hurt Nicole.

I pulled my cello from the car and pretended to adjust it in the backseat. Nicole sat back there with her cello in-between her legs. She bent over to grab a piece of paper from her book bag – a permission slip for the field trip to the symphony. Just as she looked up, my cello hit her straight in the chin – I heard the thwack from outside the car. She erupted in a loud wail. I looked into the car to see if she was okay. Secretly, I didn't care.

"Oh my god. Are you okay?" I asked.

"Ow. You did that on purpose," she said as she rubbed her chin with her hand.

"Puh-lease," I said and got myself settled into the backseat with my cello.

"Are you girls okay back there?" Nicole's mom asked.

"I think so," Nicole said.

"Yeah," I said. I sat back against the seat and stared at the houses as we pulled away from the curb. It was almost dark out as we rode home – another thing I hate about January. There are so few hours of daylight and we have to spend them all inside. It was such a crappy day. Nicole and I weren't connected like we used to be, and she became meaner over her ski vacation.

After we pulled into my driveway, Nicole's mom turned to us.

"Girls. Is everything okay with you? I didn't like the tone either of you used back there."

I felt heat rise into my entire head. I'm sure I looked like a giant frozen tomato. I waited for Nicole to reply to her mother's question.

"Mom, everything's fine," she said in a sweet sign-songy voice. "It was just an accident." She smiled at me but twisted her eyes in an evil way.

"Yeah," I said and paused, my eyes on my feet. "I didn't mean to hurt you. I'm sorry. I'm just totally klutzy."

I guess her mom was satisfied with our answers because she helped me get my cello out of the car.

All the lights were on at my house, including the Christmas lights on the tree and the mantle. In the kitchen, Mom and Colin made cookies with Emma watching them arrange multi-colored sprinkles onto sugar cookies from her highchair.

I set my bulky cello against a dining room chair and pulled the layers of outerwear from my body as I walked towards the kitchen. Clothes made a breadcrumb-like trail behind me.

"Do you have to practice that thing tonight? I hate it when you do that. It sounds like fingernails on a chalkboard," Colin said.

I punched him hard in his upper arm.

"Ow. What was that for?"

"For being a jerk. Mom, didn't you adopt him from a monkey family or something? Can we return him to the zoo?"

"Mom," Colin said as he rubbed the pain out of his arm. "Why do you have to be so mean?" He said to me and stuck out his tongue.

Emma laughed.

Later I set the cello up in the living room and examined the bow. According to Mr. Knight, the music teacher, it was made from real horsehair. I was supposed to clean it with resin each time I used it to keep the hairs soft so they wouldn't break. I ran the bow across the resin and watched as the horsehair softened. I set up my music on the side table next to the couch. It was a lot harder to practice when I couldn't see the music, let alone read it. But not many people had music stands in their house, not even Kelly.

I tuned my strings. I knew what the note was supposed to sound like when I played it, but I could never remember what the note was.

I pinched what I thought might be a chord and let the bow echo across the strings. I felt the sound inside my chest, it resonated deep in me. It sent shivers through me and gave me goose bump arms. I stared out the window and wondered where Dad was. Usually he'd be home by now. It's dark and cold and he works outside all day. He should be hungry right? Plus, wasn't he supposed to take down the Christmas tree?

Ever since Emma was born, he seemed to come home later and later. I just assumed he worked more because there were more of us kids. And, I often heard him come home late, way past when I'd gone to bed.

Sometimes he'd come into my room to kiss Colin and me on the forehead. He smelled like dried sweat and beer. I pretended to be asleep, even when I really wanted to tell him about my day, or something I'd learned. Most of the time I worried about Mom, she seemed lonely and tired.

I woke up in the middle of the night to a crash sound. It came from the living room. I sat up in bed to catch my breath – fear raced inside me. Was it a burglar? Or maybe even the boogie man.

I pulled my robe from the side of the bed and checked on Colin. He was fast asleep. I opened my bedroom door. The light in the hallway was dim. I tiptoed toward the dining room, past the framed drawings of rainbows and fire trucks Colin and I had made when we were younger. I heard Mom and Dad in the living room. Mom cried as Dad yelled at her. I crouched behind a dining chair so they couldn't see me.

I hated it when they fought. I bit my nails as I watched and listened unnoticed.

"I said you gotta learn to trust me Candice. You gotta listen to me and trust me."

"How can I trust you when you spend all our money at the bars? Grow up. You've got a family here."

"I don't need you to tell me what I got." He slumped into the big black chair. Mom stood over him. He grabbed her hand. "Let's go to bed."

"I've been in bed already." She shook his hand away and whispered. "Do you realize it's almost four? When were you planning to come home? You make me sick."

She turned to leave, and he pulled her back toward him. She stumbled and almost fell. "If I were you, I wouldn't talk to me that way. If I were you, I'd know what's good for me."

"Well, if I were you, I'd start realizing really quick that my wife is about to leave me."

I gasped and held back my urge to yell at them both to stop.

"You wouldn't."

"Try me. "Mom was speaking in a tone I'd never heard her use and it made my heart still. "I'll take the kids to Madison. We can be gone by daylight."

Mom sobbed. I wanted to run to her. I wanted to hug her and tell her everything was going to be all right. I shivered and wrapped myself in my robe. I leaned against the wall behind the table and closed my eyes. I felt the muscles in my fist clench and knew that if Dad hit her, I'd pounce on him and bash his face in.

Mom cried some more, and Dad fell asleep in his chair. I heard his snores even after I tiptoed back to my bed.

I wondered what to do. I wished I could call Papa or wake up Colin. I wished I was at Nicole's house instead of here. But I was mad at her and it was too late to call Papa or wake up Colin. I closed my eyes and pretended I didn't hear anything.

The next morning, I felt all groggy. I sat comatose at the breakfast table. I cursed Mom under my breath for nudging me awake with a sweet tone that she used to pretend she was all right. I hated her for hiding herself from me.

Dad was at the table with the paper and his coffee. He had a slim white bandage across the length of his left eyebrow and a black and red cut on his lip.

"What happened?" I asked.

Colin waddled in and sat down in front of a soggy bowl of cheerios.

"Car accident," he said. He straightened the paper with a snap.

"What?" Although I didn't get a good look at him last night, he didn't appear bloody or mangled from under the table.

"Your father was in a car accident last night. He totaled his truck. And, as you can see, he totaled his face," Mom said as she wiped Emma's mouth with her bib.

"What happened, Dad," Colin asked. He shoveled the last of the Cheerios into his mouth.

I stared into my bowl and pushed my Cheerios around in the milk. Suddenly, I didn't feel so hungry.

"Yes. Stuart, why don't you tell your children what happened," Mom said.

She got Emma from her highchair and held her on her hips. She stood over the table and stared at Dad. A weird tension filled the room. I felt the butterflies and was afraid of what might happen. Were they going to fight again? Would Mom take us to Madison?

I allowed myself the fantasy of a new school – one where I got to be the popular girl. I'd be really nice to everyone. Not bitchy like some people I knew.

Dad coughed and looked straight at me. "Well, I was driving home after work. It was real dark out. I didn't see this car up ahead of me on the turnpike near 30th and Kessler. It pulled up right in front of me and even though I slammed on my brakes, I still ran into the back of the guy's car. He's okay. But I got a little banged up."

"Did they call an ambulance?" Colin asked.

Mom pulled a chair from the table and sat down to hold Emma over her shoulder. Emma burped.

"No. I called a buddy of mine; this guy knows all sorts of medical tricks. He patched me up and helped me take care of some details."

"Where's your truck?" Colin asked.

"Shit. That reminds me. I can't drive you all to school today, Molly. Your Dad needs the car. Will you call Nicole's mom for me and see if she can do it?"

I looked at her like she had three heads. "But Mom, I have to get ready for school. I still have to get dressed."

"Molly. I was hoping you could help me out here." She looked Dad in the eye. "Now that your Dad can't."

"He can make a phone call and drive?"

"Sorry honey. I have to get going. I'm late." Dad said.

Mom gave Dad a little punch in the arm as she left the room without another word.

I crossed my arms across my chest. Colin left the table. I really wanted to go write in my journal, but I didn't have time.

I glared at Dad. He took a last sip of coffee as he stood up. I wanted to throw my body across the table and attack him for hurting Mom, me, our family, his truck, himself. Why did he have to be such a jerk? I hated him and, in that moment, vowed to hate him forever.

"Get up, Molly." His drawl was like fingers on a chalkboard. "You better get yourself ready for school."

I slammed the chair back under the table, then baby-stepped to the kitchen to dial Nicole's number. I let the blood in my veins cool. Her mom answered.

"Can you drive us all to school today?"

"Is everything all right? You sound upset."

"No, I'm fine," I put on my grown-up voice, "It's just that my mom is really sick today."

"Oh dear. Does she need any help with the baby? I could get someone   to   take   my   shift."

"No," I cut her off. "I think my dad's gonna take the day off."

As I hung up, I hated to lie. I wondered if Dad even knew how to care for a little baby. I wondered if he'd be able to do it if he had to in an emergency. I didn't think he could. He couldn't even fix his own breakfast.

At school I lugged my cello up the long wooden staircase to Room 12. Nicole practically skipped ahead of me with hers. Exhausted, I struggled to keep my eyes open during the dictionary reading and that was usually my favorite part of the day.

I was so tired that I fell asleep during our math lesson. I woke up with a pit of drool all over my arm and my desk. I wiped the spit from my face and felt the slush of my sleep, the heaviness of my body. The room was blurry. I rubbed my eyes.

"Eww. Gross," Melissa said from the desk next to mine. "Try not to drool so much next time." She rolled her eyes. "You snored too."

Ms. Byers stood above me, concerned. I really wanted her to yell at Melissa. Make her stop bugging me. But she just tapped my desk with a pencil as she moved to the back of the class.

When the lunch bell rang, I overheard Kevin and Mark laughing at Melissa's boobs and it made me smile. Kids picked up their lunch bags and got in line for lunch. I realized I didn't have lunch or lunch money. Mom totally forgot and with all the commotion of the morning I didn't think to ask her for it. I was more worried Nicole's mom would know I lied to her.

I looked to Nicole. She laughed with Mike Spangler. When he left her to meet up with Mark and Kevin in line, I approached her. I decided to give up being mad at her so I could have some lunch.

"I think I forgot my lunch today. I can't find it."

"Melissa said you were drooling during Math. That's really nasty Molly." Nicole looked over her shoulder. The line of kids moved out the door. I felt like crying. The bell rang again. I jumped inside.

"I couldn't sleep last night. So, can I share lunch or what?" My throat felt tight. I didn't want to cry in front of her. Then she'd know something was wrong.

"I'm sitting with Mike."

"Okay. I'll sit with you guys. Do you have anything good like crumb cakes?"

"Molly," Nicole gave me a doe-eyed look that said get-a-grip. "I'm sitting with Mike. Not you and Mike."

"Oh. I just thought we could share lunch like usual."

"You don't have anything to share."

She left and joined Melissa and Kelly in line. Lisa skipped up to join them. They were all so happy. I felt like I really needed to cry, so I asked Ms. Byers for a hall pass to the bathroom. I walked to the one on the second floor, the furthest from the lunchroom.

Once I locked myself in a stall, I put the top of the toilet seat down so I could sit with my knees hugged into my chest. I didn't want anyone to recognize my feet. Once I felt safe, I let it out.

I cried. I cried so hard, I gulped for air. My eyes felt burnt and my tears fell onto my shirt. I cried for my anger towards Nicole and our confusing friendship. I cried because Emma got more attention than me. I cried because Melissa saw me drool and Dad wrecked his truck and his face, because I couldn't play the cello or read sheet music. I cried because I didn't know what I'd done to make everyone hate me.

I thought about dying. What if I died right in this bathroom and they found me with puffy eyes? What if they discovered I drowned in my own tears? I tried to relax. I dried my eyes with toilet paper. I unlocked the stall and found I was still alone in the bathroom. I took a few stiff brown paper towels from the dispenser in the wall, wet them in the sink and went back into the stall to hold them over my eyes.

I took a deep breath. The bell rang again. Lunch was over. I had to face them sometime. Words ran through my head as I tried to erase the evidence of my tears. Push through. Push through.

In my head I saw butterflies breaking out of cocoons. The same images I had plastered all over my walls despite the invasion of Colin's sports car posters. Push through became my motto. I felt I had a purpose. I was to push through at all costs. And that very moment, it meant I must push my way through the doors to the bathroom and to the gym where everyone was at recess without me. They probably didn't even notice I was gone.

My sneakers were in the coat closet in Room 12, so I ran upstairs. I wanted to sneak in and grab them before anyone could see me. But Ms. Byers caught me as I walked in.

There was a thermos on her desk and the room smelled like tomato soup. A paperback in her hands looked like one of the books we read in class.

"Well, hello, Molly," she said and removed her classes. "Shouldn't you be at recess?"

"I forgot my Keds."

"Oh, well put them on and run along."

I found them in my cubby and was just about to run downstairs when Ms. Byers stopped me at the door.

"Is everything all right dear? You're usually so alert. One of my best students. Always with your hand up."

"Yeah. Fine. I just didn't sleep enough sleep last night."

"Is everything okay at home?"

"Sure," I said and gave her a can-I-go-now stare.

"You know Molly, it's none of my business, but I've noticed that you and Nicole aren't, shall I say, giggling so much these days. Haven't caught you two passing notes lately. Do you need to talk about it?"

I felt the tears burn my eyes again, but I decided to just push through, out of the conversation.

"No. Everything's great. She's just really into Mike right now."

"Girls should never pass up her friends for a boy. I suggest you remember that."

"Okay. Can I go now?"

She smiled and, with a swoosh of her hand, opened the doorway.

In the muggy gym, Mike and most of the boys played basketball, while some girls jumped rope. Nicole sat alone on the bleachers. She watched the basketball game.

I had to admit, Ms. Byers had a pretty good idea. I deserved better than Nicole's behavior. We'd been best friends since kindergarten, and I didn't want a boy to come between us.

"Hey," I said.

She grabbed my hands and pulled me into her. "Where have you been?"

"Nowhere. Just in the bathroom."

"Lisa and Melissa had a big fight. You totally missed it. Lisa slapped Melissa with the jump rope. Melissa ran to Ms. Garth. Now they're at the principal's office." Nicole's eyes lit up. I couldn't believe she was acting like nothing happened between us.

"I wish I saw it." I let go of her hands and looked her in the eyes. "Why didn't you share your lunch with me? I really didn't have anything to eat. You hurt my feelings."

"I'm sorry. It's just that…"

Kevin and Mark interrupted us. "Look at you. Like lovebirds holding hands." Kevin said.

"Pulease," I said. I stared him down like I'd seen Kristi do once.

"Leave us alone." Nicole said.

"Are you talking about your boobies or your periods?" Mark asked.

"Eww, you're foul," Nicole answered.

"Screw you," I said. I'd heard that phrase in a movie my dad liked.

"Why don't you make us," Kevin said.

They moved in close and pinned us to the bleachers. I looked behind them for a teacher. No one was around.

"Ow, stop. You're hurting me," I said. I felt the blood rush to my face. My face turned red.

"Yeah. Quit. I'm smooshed," Nicole said.

The boys pushed harder and put their hands on our chests. Mark on Nicole. Kevin on me.

"Stop it or I'm gonna tell," I said. I felt like I wanted to punch him, but I couldn't get free. I was tired from crying and I was scared.

"We're just playing Molly. Jeez," Mark said.

"Quit." Nicole said. She tried to wrestle away from him.

They pulled back and I felt a rush from the release of Kevin's hands on me. I bent over my knees to catch my breath.

"Creeps," I said at their backs.

Kevin whipped around and punched me in the gut. I fell into my knees and clutched my stomach in my hands. Nicole ran after them and yelled for Ms. Garth.

The rest is a blur. I do remember Ms. Garth. She helped me to my feet. Nobody had ever hit me like that. It really hurt. It felt like fish swam in my belly and warm acid filled my throat.

"What happened?" Ms. Garth asked, as I laid on the white bed in the nurse's office.

"Kevin hit me." I wrapped myself into a ball.

"I don't see Kevin doing a thing like that. He seems like such a sweet boy. I know his mother," said Mrs. Wayne, the nurse.

Ms. Garth shook her head at the nurse. "Now Molly, think. Did you say or do anything to provoke him?"

"No." I couldn't believe she said that. "He just wouldn't leave us alone."

"Who?"

"Me and Nicole. He and Mark kept touching us. They wouldn't quit."

"Where were they touching you," asked Mrs. Wayne. She held a warm washcloth to my forehead.

"Here." I pointed to my mostly flat chest.

"Goodness," Mrs. Wayne said.

Ms. Garth sighed and asked me to sit up. She took my hands and leaned in close. When she spoke, her breath smelled like dirty rags left in an attic. "Did they lift up your shirt?"

"No." I stood up. "I want to go back to class."

"Are you sure you're ready dear? You can always stay here as long as you need or call your mom if you want," said Mrs. Wayne.

I thought of Mom home with Emma and mad at Dad, who had the car. Was she packing her bags for Madison? "No. I just want to go upstairs."

I didn't want the nurse to know my stomach hurt, so I pretended I didn't feel a thing. Ms. Garth walked me upstairs.

"Are you sure you want to go back in there?"

"Yeah." I took in her hugeness and uni-boob. We stood in front of the closed door to the classroom. "Are Kevin and Mark in trouble?"

"Don't you worry about them. They've already had a good talking to."

"Really?" I wanted them to get expelled.

"Like I said, don't worry." When she opened the door, everyone looked at me. Ms. Byers smiled. I felt like I'd been gone the whole day.

"Our little patient is feeling better," Ms. Garth said, way too loud.

"Wonderful," said Ms. Byers. "Go ahead and take your seat dear."

I walked to our group table with my head up and sat down right across from Mark. I gave him a fake smile. He looked down at his social studies book.

"Now. Where were we?" Ms. Byers asked.

In the car on the way home from school, Nicole and I sat close together like we shared a secret. When her mom asked how our day was, Nicole told her what happened. Her mom stopped the car, pulled to the side of the road and turned around to look at us in the back seat.

"Are you okay? Were they disciplined?" She yanked up the emergency brake.

"Ms. Garth said they would be," I answered. I was glad someone outside the school knew.

"I should call all their parents," Mrs. Carr said.

Nicole wriggled next to me. "Maybe we should just wait to see if they get in trouble or not."

"I'd rather we made sure their parents knew."

That night, on the phone, Nicole and I agreed that it was a bad idea to call their parents. But we couldn't do anything about it. Her mom had already called.

15

One week after Kevin hit me, the class went on a field trip to the symphony. We were all told, in advance, to dress in a nice outfit – one we might wear to church or a to a nice dinner out with our parents. Since I never went to church or out to eat with my parents, I decided to wear the black velvet dress I wore to my uncle's wedding the last winter. It was a little too small. I had to suck in my belly when Mom helped me zip it. When I sat down, I felt it pull across my shoulders. It was totally uncomfortable. But I had no choice. Mom said "no" when I asked her for a new outfit.

"You'll just have to make do." She said. "And we may need to put you on a diet."

I stuck my tongue out at her when she turned away. I love food, I thought. It makes me feel good.

At school, I was surprised to see most of the boys in jackets with ties. Kevin's sweaty hair stuck to his face and Will wore his jacket tied around his waist; his shirt tails over his pants. Will was so cute.

The girls looked like princesses in party dresses. Everyone except Jane. I wondered if she forgot it was the day of the symphony. She wore chords and a bandanna over her hair. I felt bad for her, but I didn't ask her why she was dressed that way. I was just glad I wore the right thing.

I knew everyone would rush to sit next to their friends on the bus and I really wanted to sit next to Nicole, so I passed her a note the day before and asked her. I was so glad she said yes. Since the boys attacked us, we were joined again.

We boarded the bus in front of the school. It was freezing outside, and the bus felt muggy and smelled like old gym shoes. Mark held his nose and pretended to gag when he boarded. But, with the excitement of the field trip, no one else really cared about smells or how cold or hot it was. We just made room for everyone with their coats and scarves.

Nicole brought a book of MadLibs in her tote bag and we started to play as soon as the bus got going. When the MadLib called for a verb, we'd write *poop* or *kiss*. We loved when it called for a person in the room or a body part – then we liked to use *penis*, or *lips* or *boobs*. We giggled.

Will and Kevin sat directly behind us and played tic-tac-toe on the frozen window. When they finished a game, they'd wait the few minutes it took for the window to freeze over then play again. Pretty soon most kids were writing messages or playing hangman on the windows. The bus driver never said a word, so no one stopped. When Nicole and I got sick of the MadLibs, we drew smiley faces and flowers on ours.

Mark sat in front of us with Bret and they made spit balls with crumbled pieces of notebook paper. I don't know where they got the straw, but they took turns blowing spit balls into the back of the bus – toward Kevin and Will – so Ms. Byers, who was at the front of the bus, wouldn't see them.

It was totally gross to think of Mark and Bret's spit flying across the bus, so I told them so.

"That's nasty. Nobody wants your spit."

"Nobody wants yours either, lardass."

"What did you call me?"

"You heard me, tub of goo."

"Don't egg him on Molly," Nicole said.

"But, he's a jerk." I said, loud enough for him to hear.

"I know, but don't mess with him." She tried to get me to draw with her on the window. But I didn't want to. I was too mad and tired of all this stuff. It was so stupid.

"Yeah. Do as she says. Don't mess with me."

I cringed at his words.

Lisa and Melissa sat across the aisle and heard the whole thing. Melissa whispered to Lisa who whispered to Kevin – like a long, stupid whisper line. I had a feeling they were talking about me. A few minutes later, Kevin wrote, *Molly is putrid* on his window. He wrote it once regular so all the kids could see and once backwards so people driving by could read it. A bunch of people laughed because it had been our word of the day and they all knew what it meant. Melissa, I noticed, laughed the loudest.

I jumped up so my knees were on the seat. I bent over Nicole and Will to erase it with the palm of my hand just as Ms. Byers walked up behind me. She grabbed the collar of my coat and yanked me back into my seat.

"Young ladies do not sit like hooligans when they wear pretty dresses."

"I'm sorry, but Kevin…"

"Kevin?" She looked at him with a mean glare.

"I didn't do anything." He sat perfectly still with his wet fingers folded in his lap.

I boiled with anger because he always seemed to get away with stuff. As far as I knew, he and Mark never got in trouble for what they did to Nicole and me. I wanted Kevin to get into trouble.

"He wrote something about me on the window," I said.

"Really? What did he write?"

"Molly is putrid" someone's voice sang from the front of the bus.

I sunk lower in my seat, afraid everyone would see my red-hot cheeks.

"Kevin," Ms. Byers put her hand on his shoulder and gave him the look of death. "Is that what you wrote?"

"No."

"I'm going to ask you once more. It's your last opportunity to tell me the truth. Did you write that on the window?"

"I said, no."

Will sat motionless next to him and stared straight ahead. Nicole sat still next to me. I could hear her breath. If I had a knife, I could cut the air with it like a slice of cheese. The whole bus was silent – watching.

Ms. Byers fastened the top button of her coat, "Molly and Kevin. I'd like to see you both when we stop at the theater."

I glared at her with a tear down my cheek. I wanted her to believe me and I didn't want to get in trouble.

"Okay," I said, then sniffled.

Mark turned to me when she went back to the front of the bus. "You're gonna get it for being such a lard ass."

"Shut up, idiot," Nicole said.

"Yeah, we'll see who gets in trouble, turd face."

"Ooh, burn," Nicole laughed. But it wasn't a happy laugh.

Well at least she was on my side, I thought. I just couldn't bear it if she wasn't.

The bus stopped in front of a massive limestone building. There were other buses and hundreds of kids walking up the steps. I felt my stomach clench into a ball. I thought I might be sick. Where was the nurse when I needed her? I waited with Ms. Byers for Kevin to get off the bus. He was the last one. Such a wimp. I hated him. Rich punk. My hands were fists in my coat pockets.

Once our class went up the stairs to the Symphony, Ms. Byers gave us her speech. "I've just about had enough of you both. Disrupting class. Hurting one another. Throwing insults."

"But I, he …" I tried to tell her it wasn't me. It was him. I didn't do anything.

"No, I've heard enough from you both. Now. I want to see each of you at my desk during recess tomorrow and for the rest of the week."

"Aww," Kevin said.

"Why?" I asked.

"I think you two need to learn how to appreciate one another."

"We do?" I looked at Kevin. His head was down.

"Yes. I think you would really like each other given a chance."

I thought I'd puke. I'd never like Kevin.

Because we were so late, everyone was already seated inside. Bret, Will, and Mark saved a seat for Kevin. I spotted Nicole in-between Lisa and Melissa. She looked at me and shrugged her shoulders. I had to sit in the back row with Ms. Byers.

The symphony began with a loud crash of cymbals and songs with the same instruments we played at school – cello, clarinet, bass, viola and drums. The sounds weren't just sounds though, they were music. I didn't think we'd ever get that good. I felt this music dance inside my chest.

Despite my love of the music, I felt so alone. For every positive thing that happened, for every one thing that I loved and felt secure about, there were five bad feelings, bad experiences, bad people around to block my happiness. I couldn't grab a hold of the good feeling long enough to save it.

Preserve it. Be it. Lock it in a box – like the one with the dancing ballerina and secret compartment. I wished I could put away my happiness and experiences like skipping or laughing with Nicole – and have them to look at, admire, and remember when I wanted to see something good, pretty and all mine.

I let the music and the dance continue in my belly. It rolled around like kids chasing each other, laughing on the playground. This felt like goodness to me. The harmless music. The spirited clarinets and soulful hum of cellos.

After school I went straight to the refrigerator and ate one of the peanut butter, wheat germ and honey balls Mom left on a plate for Colin and me. Then I ate another and another and another until there was only one left. It made me feel that happy feeling again, like at the symphony, to eat the peanut butter balls.

I sat on the couch with a bellyache and enjoyed a *Tom and Jerry* cartoon. Then Colin noticed there was only one snack left.

"Mom. Molly ate everything," he said so loud that he spoke to the whole house.

When she didn't answer, he tried again.

"Mom. Molly's a big pig. She ate all the snacks."

"I did not." I thought about Kevin calling me a lard ass. I got mad again.

"You   did   so.   I'm   telling."

"You've already told, idiot." I punched him hard in the arm.

"Ow. Mom. Molly hit me."

Mom came into the room. Her hair stuck up in the back and she struggled to put on her glasses. Large creases from her pillow marked her cheek.

"What's going on?"

"Molly ate all the snacks."

"No. Honey. I'm sure there's more in there. I made a dozen."

"They're all gone. I only got one."

"Molly. How many did you eat?"

She didn't seem to care I hit Colin, but I hid my face in the couch cushion. "I don't know." I mumbled.

"Sweetie.   You'll   get   a   belly   ache."

"Oink oink." Colin said. He huffed out of the room.

Mom sat with me on the couch and rubbed her hand slowly over my back. It felt so good to be touched in a loving way. I started to cry.

"Oh, baby. What's wrong?"

"Nothing." I gulped for air under the couch pillow and dried my eyes on my sleeve. "Nobody likes me."

"Oh honey, sure they do."

I let her hold me in her arms. It felt so good and it had been a long time since she'd held me like that – like a baby who needed hugs and kisses. She held me like that for a few minutes, then dried my tears and brushed my hair back with her fingers.

"I'll make dinner. You go on and do your homework."

"I don't have any."

"Well, then go read for a while. Dinner will be ready shortly."

I went to my room and wrote in my diary.

Dear Diary,

Today Kevin said I was putrid, and everybody laughed. We both got in trouble and we have to stay in during recess tomorrow and I hate him. I also hate Lisa and Melissa and Nicole is totally on my nerves because she didn't save a seat for me at the symphony. I thought we were friends again. I thought Lisa was my friend too. What did I do to make things change between us? I don't understand why no one can make this better.

Love Always, Molly

I looked onto the page. The words seemed hardly my own, yet so familiar. I locked the diary and put the key in the secret compartment in my ballerina jewelry box.

When Mom called me for dinner, I told her I wasn't hungry, and I just wanted to read in bed. I wanted her to make an effort with me, make me come to the table with them, but she let me skip dinner. I feel asleep after she left my room.

16

ear Diary, School sucks. No one and I mean no one, not even Jane Simpson talks to me. I hate getting up in the morning and I wish I could learn at my own pace at home. I hate everyone, especially Nicole, but I wish things could be like they were. We had to read Diary of Anne Frank and even though my life isn't half as bad as hers, not even close, I still feel doomed. I can't be happy, and I don't know how to change. I wish I felt more love, Molly

For weeks, the dreary days of February and March dragged on as we tried to stay awake during the reading of the day's word and read books on our animals in the overheated Room 12. Ms. Byers made Kevin and I sit together in a special area while the rest of the class worked on their projects at their group tables. We were supposed to help each other with our talks. Rather than help though, or even work on his talk about piranhas, Kevin drew figures of space men in his notebook.

I looked out the window. It was two in the afternoon and almost dark. I looked at Jane. She sat at her group desk with a pile of butterfly books from the library, my stack was all about snakes.

Kevin looked at me over his spaceman on the moon drawing.

"You know, my brother has a snake. Name's Harold."

"A snake named Harold," I said. "What kind is he?"

"A boa constrictor."

"No way."

"Yah way. And, he doesn't even have a cage. He just lives in his room."

I got goosebumps and shivered at the idea. "Eww."

"He's really nice. Sometimes I get to feed him."

"Does he eat mice?" I asked. I learned that from my book.

Kevin nodded. "And, hamsters."

"Why did he name him Harold?"

"After our step-dad." Kevin looked down at his paper and started to draw again.

"Does he care?" I wouldn't want a snake named after me.

"He doesn't live with us anymore."

"Oh," I said. Not sure what to say.

"Yeah, I didn't even like him so I'm glad."

Besides playing with Colin, that was the longest conversation I'd ever had with a boy. I thought maybe Kevin had problems too. Maybe we were becoming friends.

Later at lunch Nicole grabbed my hand as I stood in line by myself.

"What's up with you and Kevin?"

"Nothing." She had this tone I didn't like. I'd never heard her talk like that, only Melissa. I hated that Melissa was rubbing off on her.

"Do you like him?"

I thought about Kevin and his silly spaceman drawings and his step-dad snake name.

"No."

"I saw you talk to him today, so I was just wondering."

"I know. I have to. We work on our reports together."

She squinted her eyes and held my hand like we were best friends again. I could tell she wanted me to say something else. But I didn't know what to tell her. I was sad that she'd become like them – like the girls I couldn't talk to.

"It's not like you want to go with him, right Molly?"

"God no." I made a blech sound. Nicole laughed. I laughed too.

"Good," she said. "Cause Melissa would be mad."

"Why do you care so much?"

"I don't know. Melissa just knows them best."

I walked away from her and sat down by myself at the lunch table. Jane sat by herself at another table. She looked uncomfortable in her own skin. I didn't want to become her. I still kinda wanted to be like them, but better.

17

Finally, Spring started to arrive. Little green flower leaves poked up through the dirt in our side yard. The smell of drying rain and lilies of the valley made me happy. For days, it rained cats and dogs. And each of those rainy days we had to spend recess indoors. The teachers would set up craft areas in the fluorescent lunchroom and we were encouraged to have creative art time. I enjoyed the indoor playtime; it soothed me. It felt like a relief to be alone and not run around playing eraser tag.

Over the last weeks, I'd distanced myself more and more from the girls. Rather than try to be friends, or fit in, I stayed to myself and enjoyed whatever time Nicole gave me when she wasn't flirting with Mike Spangler or laughing with Kelly, Melissa and Lisa. It seemed everyday Melissa was mad at Lisa or Kelly, but never at Nicole. And, I didn't want to get involved. It wasn't fun to be on Melissa's mad-at-you-side.

Nicole told me she'd held Mike Spangler's hand once. And, she said it felt like lightening on her arm. Lisa talked to me every once in a while, because our moms became friends. But I think maybe her mom made her do it. She didn't talk to me natural. But always like she already knew me, not the kids at my old school or even Nicole before she became weird, but like she didn't really want to hear what I had to say. It felt funny, like a square peg in a round hole. We didn't fit.

Mark dumped Melissa and that surprised me. I didn't think I'd ever see her upset at school like she got. She huddled in a corner of the cafeteria one day with Lisa, Kelly and Nicole at her side. I think she cried. But I couldn't tell. I wanted her to be sad too. So, I imagined she did.

One day the sun broke through the clouds, finally, and we were allowed a recess outside. As the doors burst open after lunch, my class, along with the other fifth and sixth graders ran around the playground. Free at last.

Nicole was home sick, so I was really on my own. I walked alone to the jungle gym where I liked to do my tricks on the bars. I was midway through a somersault over the bar when Lisa approached.

"What'cha you doing?" She stood with her hands on her hips. Her head cocked to watch me upside down.

"Not much." I tried to see if she was alone. But it was hard upside down.

"We've been talking, and we want to let you be our friend."

"What do you mean?" I finished with a mock Olympic dismount and faced her and the concrete slab of the kickball field. I giggled inside and felt butterflies. I'm good at the jungle gym, I thought to myself.

"We've decided you can be our friend if you just go through an initiation first."

"What kind of initiation?" I felt heat rise in my chest and my heart beat faster. Wet palms again, I rubbed them on my jeans. The air felt thick.

Lisa turned and my eyes followed her.

Kelly and Melissa huddled together with a Chinese jump rope. They looked up and came over.

Melissa spoke first. "We've decided that if you beg to be our friend, we'll let you in."

A wave of sharp panic washed over me. I felt my cheeks go red and the butterflies were back in full force. They flew around my stomach. I really wanted them to stop teasing and ignoring me and figured what would it hurt, really, just to do what they asked? I remembered my words to myself at the slumber party when they put lotion in my hair. Could I trust them? How would I push through this time?

"No way!" I turned from the group and crossed my arms over my chest and tried to hold back the tears that rimmed my eyes.

"Come on. We promise we'll be nice after you do it," Melissa said. "Yeah." All the girls chimed in.

I faced them all again. I looked at each of the girls. Melissa glared with her hips cocked, hands in the pockets of her corduroys. Kelly ran her fingers through her long, thick brown hair and her long eyelashes closed over her eyes as she blinked. Lisa looked over her shoulder at Kevin and Mark who were chasing each other with a handful of sand. She had one hand over her mouth, the other adjusting the straps of her sundress. Her cheeks raised and her eyes bugged out.

I knew I just hated them all for every whisper and mean thing. Yet, that one part of me still felt like I did on the first week of school -- I wanted to be them all. I felt my knees bend and then hit the sand. I felt heavy as I lifted my gaze toward the girls and raised my hands in mock prayer like I'd seen cowboys do in the movies when they begged for the bad guy to save them. They always had a trick up their sleeve to save the day. Maybe I'd find one too.

The words just flew out of my own mouth.

"Please, please won't you be my friends."

Then the rest of the afternoon melted into a stream of slow-motion images.

Lisa, Melissa and Kelly laughed.

I ran to the bathroom with "We're just kidding. We wanted to see how far you'd go" echoing in my head.

I sat in music class. I couldn't move my bow.

I bit my nails as I watched the clock on the wall and waited for Mom to pick me up from school and for the day to be over.

I sat in the back seat with thoughts of ice cream, ding dongs and popsicles in my head. I was so mad. Once in our driveway, I opened the door before the car came to a complete stop, got out, slammed the door behind me and ran into the house. I slammed the front door, ran straight to my room, threw myself onto my bed and cried.

Dear Diary,

Today was THE absolute WORST day of my life. EVER. I am so mad. I am humiliated. I feel weak. Puny. Like a bug. An ant that someone steps on without even thinking about. Is this what it feels like to be a human?

First, I had a terrible morning trying to figure out what to wear. It was like I hated everything in my closet, and I was super mad at Mom and Dad because I haven't gotten new clothes since the fall, and now I have to wear all the same spring clothes as last year. I hate it all. But that's not the worst of it.

After already feeling like I'll never fit in with all those snotty rich kids who I shouldn't even feel like I want to be like anyways because they're all jerks, I had a totally horrible experience at the playground over recess that I'm sure everyone at school will be talking about into infinity. I'm scared to even say it. I feel dirty. But the worst of it is that Melissa, Lisa and Kelly made me beg to be their friend and I did it. Then they told me they were just kidding.

I'm crying right now and will probably soak this paper.

When I got home from school all I wanted to do was cry and be left alone – but no, Mom had to come out of her baby land trance and catch me eating a big block of cheddar and tell me that she's worried I'm gaining weight! I'm so angry, like I don't even care. She wanted to sit down and have a talk and try to get deep with me. "Really connect," she said. Oh, and I'm supposed to just say "You know Mom, my life sucks right now and all I want to do is eat. Will you give me a hug?"

But instead, I slammed the refrigerator door so hard she told me to "watch it." And, I stomped in here and threw my math homework against the wall. I guess Mom decided to stay away because she hasn't knocked on my door in a while.

I'm just so tired. I'm tired of crying. Tired of trying so hard all the time. I bet if I got really sick no one would even care. I don't want to go to school tomorrow.

My hand is tired and shaky, and I just hope I have good dreams tonight because it's been the worst day ever. Molly

We ate dinner without Dad again. Mom said he had to work late. I pushed the Chef Boyardee raviolis around my plate. For the first time in forever I wasn't hungry at dinner. Maybe I'll starve to death, I thought.

Colin sat across from me and tickled Emma's bare feet as she sat in her highchair next to him. Mom didn't sit still, she kept getting up to clean the kitchen and put her hands on the sink and stare out the window. She didn't even notice that I was sad.

"Quit that." I said to Colin when he made Emma giggle again. "I have a headache."

"So," he said and tickled her again.

I hated their happiness. I wanted it too, but I felt stuck in my sad mad. I wanted to be pulled up, but there was no one to help.

I threw my napkin at him.

"Quit," he said. "Mom, Molly won't leave me alone."

"Leave him alone, Mol." Mom yelled from the kitchen.

She came back to the table to pick up Emma.

"What's gotten into you two? You used to be friends."

That sounds familiar I thought.

"Nothing," I said. "He just bugs me."

"You're so mean," Colin said.

"I am not." I felt the anger inside me again.

"Why don't you two finish up so we can watch *Six Million Dollar Man* before bed."

"I don't want to," I said as I got up from the table.

"Fine," Mom said.

"Fine," I said.

And, then I went to bed. Mad and sad again.

I got up early so I could read *Stranger with my Face* before school. I was really into the story and wanted to lay in bed reading all day.

As I sat in the bed, I listened to the house wake up around me. I heard Mom in the kitchen, the clank of coffee mugs, Dad's voice and the snap and crinkle of his morning paper. I really wanted to make the morning last. I snuggled into the covers and turned over on my side to lie with my knees hugged into my chest and held the book next to my face.

I wished I could astral project like the girls in the book and send my soul into the cosmos to find another body to inhabit. Another's life to live. I knew for sure that no one would want to come and steal my body and life right now. I didn't even want to get out of bed for school.

I could already feel the cold stares of my classmates. By now, I was sure everyone knew about the begging. I felt humiliated. Why couldn't something, anything, go right? I had thought this would be a good school year. I was at a school for smart kids. I got to read books I really liked, make creative projects and I liked my teacher. So why was everything going wrong? I couldn't put my finger on what I'd done to make everyone hate me and didn't have a clue how to change the fact that everyone would surely know what happened on the playground.

"Come on sleepy head. You're gonna be late for school," I heard Mom say as she tapped on the door.

I sank deeper into the bed. I'll just play sick today, I thought. I coughed into my pillow, just as Mom came into the room.

"What's going on? You're not even dressed?"

"My stomach hurts. I have rickets."

"Darling. You don't have rickets."

"Get up. Let's go." She snapped her fingers.

"I can't. They'll all laugh."

She sat on my bed and looked at me, deep inside.

"What do you mean?"

"I told you before. Nobody likes me."

"Oh, sweetie. Of course, they do. What makes you say that?" She ran her fingers through my hair, and I felt myself folding inside. I wanted more.

"They just don't. I know it." I felt a tear. I just couldn't tell her what happened. It was too hard to say. It wouldn't even come out of my mouth.

"Well you can have a day off if you really need it, but I think you should go. Be strong, sweeties. You're a Greely. We're strong people."

"Mom. I can't. I'm scared."

"Molly, there is nothing to be afraid of. I know you can do this, and I promise you, everything will be all right?"

I felt that familiar burn in my chest and just knew I'd cry.

"Look, I'll let you think about what you want to do over the next five minutes. But then I need to know because I have to call Claudia and tell her you won't need a ride. Ok?"

"Ok," I said, barely audible.

I clenched my fists under the sheets. I let out a big silent scream under my breath. My whole body tightened in hatred, for them and myself. Then my muscles relaxed, and I said to myself, "I promise I will never let them hurt me again. I promise they will never hurt me again. They will never hurt me again. From this day on, I will be smarter, quicker, funnier, better and I will never let them in again. They cannot have me. I will not let them in. I hate them all. I will push through."

I got out of bed, dressed in my favorite jumper and rainbow turtleneck and my best blue striped socks and went to the kitchen for breakfast.

Nicole gave me a quiet smile when I got into the car. I noticed she had a cast on her arm all the way from her wrist above her elbow. Her arm bent in a permanent L-shape.

"What happened?" No one I knew ever had a cast before.

"I fell off the back-porch stairs playing with Teddy."

"Does it hurt?" I felt love for her. I wanted her to be okay.

"Not anymore. But it did at first."

"She was a very brave girl," Mrs. Carr said from the driver's seat.

"I have to wear it for twelve whole weeks."

"Wow." I didn't know what to say. Maybe she didn't know what happened at the playground. "Can I sign it?"

"Sure." She handed me a big purple marker. "Dad gave it to me so everyone could do it."

I added my name with a smiley face in the "O".

We walked up to the second-floor classroom together. I took a deep breath and entered Room 12. I thought for sure everyone would stare at me. But they didn't even notice me. Everyone gathered around Nicole and her cast like they were superstars. Maybe they forgot. I thought. Something good.

18

was super scared to do my talk. The night before I ate an extra bowl of ice cream for dessert and gave myself a bellyache – hoping to be sick the next day. But I was really prepared, and I was really ready, so I knew I shouldn't worry.

I When Kevin and I got into trouble after the symphony, Ms. Byers made us spend two whole weeks helping each other research our talks. I actually learned a lot about snakes from Kevin. I wasn't even scared of them anymore because they were usually pretty lazy unless you poked them with a stick or something to make them mad. Kevin and I got along pretty okay when we studied together. When he was on his own, he was nice. It was just when he was with other boys – like Mark– he could be a real jerk. He reminded me of a snake, actually. When he was treated with kindness – when he was left alone to do his own thing, he was tame, like a snake alone in the woods who hurt no one. But when he was provoked, especially by other guys, he could be like a poisonous monster who would hurt anything that got in his way.

During my research, I learned a lot about how snakes shed skin. Most fascinating was that after a certain period of time snakes shed the old to reveal the new. I also read somewhere that this old skin contained old cells– the molting of snakes revealed new cells, new growth. New snakes altogether.

And, while I was still mad that Jane got to do the report on butterflies, I found myself liking snakes. Like butterflies they are able to camouflage themselves to hide from predators. Some hid on trees, others in sands of deserts. And like butterflies, they are everywhere.

It's just that I couldn't shake the idea that snakes were bad, and butterflies were good. That to do my report on butterflies was good and to have to do it on snakes was bad. Like a compromise – like I was forced to do it. It was like the cello. I was okay at it, but it wasn't natural for me. I could understand it, but I wasn't going to be in a symphony. Maybe I'd try the drums next year, I thought, something new.

The day we started to do our talks, most everyone brought white poster boards covered with plastic trash bags. Kelly unwrapped hers – she drew all the horses by hand and colored them in with marker and colored pencils. It made me feel like mine wasn't good enough – just paper cut outs from an old *National Geographic* glued onto the board.

The butterflies danced their familiar dance in my belly as Ms. Byers drew names from a hat of all the people who would give their talks on the first day. She'd reminded us that it would take a week for the entire class to get their turn – but she gave us all a point because we all brought our finished projects in on the due date. We weren't even allowed to work on them even if our names weren't called until the very end.

My name wasn't called on that first day and I was so relieved. Melissa had to go, though. She was very nervous when she talked in front of the whole class. I could tell because she kept skipping over her words – even though we were allowed to write the whole thing on note cards. I didn't feel sorry for her. I wanted her to get a bad grade.

After school Nicole called me. It'd been a long time since she called me out of the blue. I missed her but I'd kinda gotten used to no one calling and just writing everything I wanted to say in my diary. I was surprised to hear from her. She felt so far away and different now. And, with her cast, she was a new person. Something deep changed in us both.

"What's up?" I asked.

"I just wanted to laugh with you about Melissa's report. I hope mine goes better than that."

"Why don't you call Kelly and Lisa and laugh with them?"

"They're like Melissa's best friends. No way."

"Oh, so you'll call me 'cause I'm not friends with her."

"Sort of." I twirled a piece of my hair and waited for Nicole to say something else.

"It was sort of bad wasn't it?"

"Yeah. She skipped her words like a stone in a pond."

"It sounded like she didn't even do research," Nicole said.

"Maybe not. Maybe she was busy" It felt fun to talk to Nicole. But I really didn't want to be mean like they were mean to me.

"We had almost the whole year."

"Yeah, but she's been busy being a snot." And, the minute she said it, I felt sick to my stomach and excited all at the same time.

"Totally." I thought Nicole was finally coming around to my side. "She's been so mean."

I didn't know what to say. Should I tell her about the playground? Did she already know? I was scared to say anything. Plus, I didn't want to bring it up. I wanted it to be in the past. Like forever ago or never.

"Totally." I said. And, smiled.

I had to do my talk the next day. I got nervous all over again but held my head high because I knew I was prepared. Like Nancy Drew on her brave adventure and Caddie Woodlawn on her horse, I knew I'd succeed. There was not a doubt in my head.

I was to present my ten-minute talk in the afternoon after recess and I decided that rather than do tricks on the bars, I would review my 3x5 note cards under a big dogwood tree – away from the groups of kids so I could concentrate.

Daffodil stems burst from the ground around the fence. The ground was still hard and a bit damp from winter, so I laid my jacket down and sat on top of. The air felt warmer than it had in months and I was so happy to sit under the tree before it bloomed. Change was in the air.

Melissa and Nicole walked by me and Melissa whispered in Nicole's ear. Nicole giggled, looked at me and giggled again. Melissa got up real close to me and Nicole gave her a gentle push. Her foot knocked up against my hands and my note cards flew across the dirt. My hands ached from being kicked so I ignored Melissa as I blew on them and shook them to release the pain. Melissa and Nicole ran over to Kelly and Lisa and giggled. I gathered up the last note card; they were a bit muddy, but I could still read them.

I was furious at them and ran to the bathroom to cry as quietly as I could before I had to be inside to give my talk. I didn't want anything they said or did to disrupt my confidence or my ability to deliver a talk that I'd worked really hard on and knew would be great. I thought about the snake and the butterfly again. Push through, I thought. Push through to something new.

I looked at myself in the mirror and dabbled my eyes with a wet paper towel to hide the redness. I was so tired of crying all the time.

Back in Room 12, I totally ignored them all. I didn't want to watch them pass notes or whisper in each other's ears anymore. I was past caring what they thought. I focused on doing a great talk. I reminded myself that there was a reason I was at this school and it was not to make friends or go with boys or giggle and pass notes. It was to get a good education so I could one day go to college and become something – like a famous photographer or a writer.

When Ms. Byers called my name, I unwrapped my white poster board with the colorful cutouts of snakes and North American habitat and admired my own neat lettering on the white background. I consulted my dirty and partly torn note cards and looked into the roomful of classmates who sat in total silence waiting for me to begin. I knew they'd all have to be quiet because when someone made gurgling noises while Jane did her report the day before, Ms. Byers told them to be quiet and Jane didn't even notice.

I began my report with a story of a poisonous snake on the prowl for his next meal and talked about how long it takes to digest a field mouse and that this particular snake would probably live to be 14 years old and six feet long. I let my voice sound excited the way I sounded when I read stories to Emma and when I made up new voices for each character. I pretended I was Nancy Drew doing a commercial for sports cars and it felt great.

When I was done, I took my poster board and my dirty note cards back to my seat, sat up straight and stared ahead. I let myself drink in my own accomplishment and gave myself a little hug inside my chest.

"Very good job, Molly. That was excellent. Very Informative." Ms. Byers said loud enough for everyone to hear her praise.

I felt like a glow surrounded me. Like I'd won the school spelling bee or the science fair. I felt like I'd done something right. I didn't even notice how the other kids reacted because, finally, I didn't care.

At the end of the day, I walked with Nicole to her mom's car. Before we stepped into the Bug, I felt a tap on my shoulder. I turned around. It was Will – with a smile.

"Hey, that was a really good talk."

"Thanks," I said. I felt my cheeks get red.

"I hope mine's as good as that. I'll probably have to go tomorrow." He put his hands in his pockets and looked toward the Catholic School across the street. Uniformed kids started to walk home too.

"I'm sure you'll be great," I said. I felt like I had reason to give encouragement. I smiled as he looked up.

He smiled back.

"Well, I gotta run. Gotta hang out with my little brother. I'm teaching him to play drums."

"Wow. I wish you could teach me." I couldn't believe I said that.

"Sure. Whenever you want." I couldn't believe he said that.

"Sweet. See ya."

"See ya."

And, I got into the car. I smiled the whole way home and forgot all about being mad at Nicole for a few minutes.

When I got home, Mom was reading on the porch and Emma played with a mess of baby toys on her blanket.

"How was school?"

"I did my report and it was great!" I told her.

"That's great baby. I'm so proud of you. Come here."

I went to her and we hugged. I felt warm and happy.

"Go have some snacks. I made oatmeal cookies."

"Thanks Mom."

I gave Emma a hug and went to my room with a cookie.

Dear Diary,

Something good happened today. I did a really good job on my report and it felt great. Then Will said Hi to me and it wasn't a big joke. It was real. It felt like a cherry on a sundae.

I stopped writing mid-thought and realized it was the first time in a very long time that I didn't cry after school, even though it wasn't a perfect day. I felt happy.

Everything's gonna be okay.
Love Molly.

19

The next day, I woke up with sore palms and knew that I had to say something to Nicole. I decided recess was as good a time as any other and sent Nicole a note during our science lesson asking her to meet me near the steps behind the lunchroom, way far away from the rest of the kids at recess. I told her to please come by herself, that I really wanted to talk to her in private. She said yes.

During lunch I barely touched the baloney sandwich with mustard Mom made me. It was one of my favorite sandwiches too. But, as I sat at the lunch table, alone in my thoughts about what I was going to say and how I was going to say it, I just tore the sandwich in pieces and nibbled on little bits. My stomach seemed full of something else. I looked over to Will who sat with Bret and Mark. He didn't see me, but I felt good things, like maybe we could be friends.

Once the bell rang for recess, I walked straight for the back stairs and waited for Nicole. I'd given her a look at lunch and in between giggles with Kelly and Melissa she looked at me knowingly – like I'd seen her do tons of times. A special look that only we shared.

When she finally came skipping over to me, her pleated skirt bouncing with her, she stopped abruptly and said, "What's up?"

I sat down on the stairs and looked into my hands and off in the distance into someone's backyard behind the school. I was afraid to look her in the eyes. My belly clenched, but I'd practiced what I wanted to say, and it felt right so I just had to say it.

"Well, I'm not blind Nicole. I know you were with Melissa yesterday when she kicked the note cards from my hands and I just wanted to know why. I mean we've been friends since kindergarten and I just don't understand what happened."

I gave her a look, raised my eyebrows. She made a point with her foot as if she were doing a ballet move. Which just made me mad all over again.

"I don't know. I really don't."

"Well I think back to the beginning of the school year. We were totally excited to come to this new school together and then things changed. What changed for you?"

I felt a wave of strength wash over me.

Nicole sat down cross-legged next to me. She tucked her skirt in between her thighs. "I don't know. I just started playing with Kelly and Melissa. They'd invite me to do things. I guess they always just talk about you, so I played along."

"But why? If you're my friend, why don't you defend me? I'd defend you."

"But you don't have to. I'm not like you, Molly. I don't care about the stuff you care about."

"What do you mean? Like what?"

"Like books, or studying and stuff."

"But that's just what we have to do for school. What does that have to do with anything?"

"I don't know. It's just that you're different or something. It's easier to be with them."

"But it used to feel easy for us. Right? I mean, I always used to feel that."

"I guess. But, like you said, something's changed."

I felt myself on the verge of tears. The familiar swell in my head and eyes was almost uncontrollable, but I'd promised myself I wouldn't cry. I was done with that.

"But I don't want it to change. I liked it the way it was." I gulped in my words.

"Molly, you're so dramatic. That's what I mean. You make a big deal out of everything."

"You would too if they were mean to you."

"Maybe. I don't know."

I didn't know what else to say. I looked over at the playground and the kids from our class running around. "So, what now? I guess we're just not best friends anymore, huh?"

"Not really. But it's not like we're not friends either."

"I guess."

Nicole stood up and brushed flecks of concrete from her blue skirt "I gotta go." She skipped off towards the playground.

I felt like I'd not gotten what I wanted. I didn't know what I wanted exactly, but maybe I wanted her to remember how much fun we used to have, and I wanted our friendship back.

I sat there, on the steps, with my chin resting in my palms, bent over my legs, staring into space. I jumped when I heard the bell ring. I picked myself up and walked upstairs to the classroom where everyone was goofing off, asking Ms. Byers a question, putting lunch boxes in the coat closet – all the usual everyday stuff. I felt so on the outside looking into a new world I just couldn't seem to connect to. And, I saw Will at his desk reading a book I'd never seen before.

"Hey," I said as I approached. He looked up at me and smiled. "What are you reading?"

"Oh. It's *My Side of the Mountain*."

"What's it about?"

"A boy who runs away from home to live in the woods by himself."

"Scary."

"Not really. It sounds like a good idea. You can borrow it when I'm done."

"Okay."

Maybe I had a new friend after all. It's just not what I expected.

EPILOGUE

For the last month of school, I hung out with Will, but it wasn't like we were boyfriend and girlfriend or anything. We just liked the same stuff. And, no one teased us or anything. Not even the boys. It's like it all just stopped. The quiet after a storm. I picked up the pieces and moved on.

When school let out for the summer, Will asked if we'd still be friends and I was glad to say, "Yes."

.....

Dear Diary,

School is over and I'm so glad to be done with it. It was a really hard year. I loved that I got to read The Cay, Escape from Warsaw *and* Caddy Woodlawn *and that I got an A on my first ever research talk. But everything else was like stepping in a big pile of doggie dodo wearing my favorite patent leather shoes.*

I'm excited for summer though. I get to go to the pool everyday if I want and this summer, in addition to the regular softball league stuff, Mom said I could take tennis lessons once a week! I guess Dad got some big job and they can afford it, so I said yes! Maybe I'll make some new friends over the summer too and Will said he'd teach me to play drums. Something good will happen to me, I just know it. I still miss Nicole, but I know I'll see her at softball, so there's no escaping it. I'm so glad Melissa doesn't play. Plus, this year will be Emma's first summer and I can't wait to teach her to swim!

Love Always, Moll

63649649R10079